# This was not going to be easy

Every step, Bolan turned his efforts to spotting new opportunities, discarding lost openings and chances as they fell behind.

That was how the Executioner had survived for so long—not by being a good shot, not by being strong, not by having the biggest guns. It was having a mind as sharp as a razor, constantly keeping it in motion, like a shark on the hunt, always awake, always sniffing for traces of weakness to pounce on.

That's when he saw the red dot dance across the back of the man in the lead.

# MACK BOLAN

## The Executioner

# The Executioner®

### Don Pendleton's

## SERPENT'S LAIR

A GOLD EAGLE BOOK FROM

## W RLDWIDE.

TORONTO • NEW YORK • LONDON
AMSTERDAM • PARIS • SYDNEY • HAMBURG
STOCKHOLM • ATHENS • TOKYO • MILAN
MADRID • WARSAW • BUDAPEST • AUCKLAND

First edition February 2006
ISBN 0-373-64327-6

Special thanks and acknowledgment to
Doug Wojtowicz for his contribution to this work.

SERPENT'S LAIR

All men possess in their bodies a poison which acts upon serpents; and the human saliva, it is said, makes them take to flight, as though they had been touched with boiling water. The same substance, it is said, destroys them the moment it enters their throat.

—Pliny the Elder, 23–79
*Natural History*

All men have the strength and ability to crush the serpents that torment them. When we speak for truth and justice, our words are poison to them and it destroys them as if they have been burned by acid. To the vipers who stalk the world, my efforts are to make sure that truth defeats them wherever they are found.

—Mack Bolan

To Don, the original dragonslayer who started
Mack off tilting not at windmills, but at the real
dragons tormenting good people everywhere.
You gave us an outlet for hope of justice.

# Prologue

Doves broke from the treetops as the man in black raced among the trunks. His pursuers were fueled by a feral rage. The lone warrior reached for the gleaming silver weapon on his belt, but held it in its sheath as he broke through the tree line.

He slowly took out his katana, a long, graceful unveiling of gleaming metal. He walked toward the shore of the stagnant river, his wooden sandals scraping the smoothed river stones and gravel that rose from the edge of the water.

Enemy swordsmen raced to circle him and cut him off, but the man in black didn't make a run for it. He was in the water, six inches deep, the hem of his *hakama* soaking through. He spread his legs, keeping the tip of his sword at waist-height, both hands wrapping around the black cords on the handle.

He counted them. Eight men. He breathed deeply, resisting the urge to gulp air after the chase and battle with Zakoji's guards. Instead, he relaxed.

"You thought that you could bring death to me, intruder?" a voice called out from the tree line.

Zakoji appeared, dressed in black robes, a red serpent embroidered on the left side of his body. It was the *Uwibami*, a monsterous serpent that snatched men from horseback. It was the symbol of Zakoji's army.

"I came here seeking work," the man in black said. "Honest work."

"There can be no honest work for the henchman of the shogunate. Not the monster who reigns over these lands."

The man in black was silent. He knew that to survive, he had to be still, to sense his enemies before they even moved. Sensing that brief flash of lethal hostility had saved the warrior more than once.

With the rustle of fabric, the black-clad warrior did a quarter turn, his sword point drawing an arc that went from pointing directly in front of him to sticking out behind him like the tail of some massive scorpion. The attacking swordsman took a second step, but he was already dying before the warrior reversed his blade and sliced it across the cultist's face.

He dipped the tip of his sword into the water, letting the blood run off the hammered steel.

The circle of seven spread farther apart, to equalize the distance between them, to cut down on the intruder's ability to escape.

"He sent you. You are no *ronin*, you are still the shogun's own second! You came here at his beck and call, seeking to dip your steel in my blood.

The *ronin* shook his head, but doubted further debate would dissuade Zakoji. He knew Zakoji was a cold-blooded murderer, and his duty stated that he had to act against the savage. He cleared his mind preparing for the attack he knew would start in a heartbeat.

Steel sparked on steel as the first man made his move. The *ronin* sidestepped, avoiding a second cut from behind as he twirled the sword around, carving through the throat of the first assailant. With a pivot, he brought down his steel, slicing through the arm of the man who lunged at him from behind, the sharp belly of his blade carving through muscle and bone in an effortless movement that dropped the attacker's sword to the ground.

He dug one foot into the gravel and bowed deeply to twist under a flashing sword. The point of his katana speared the belly of a third man, guts spilling out through the massive rent in his abdomen.

The *ronin* stood up straight and flicked his sword down, deflecting a chop that lashed at his leg. The blade only snagged the black fabric and exposed the bare leg underneath.

The enemy swordsmen pressed their attack with ferocity. The warrior in black was driven into a defensive fight that he knew he could not win.

Four men were on one side of him. The fifth, though lacking an arm and swiftly losing blood, picked up his blade to continue the struggle for his lord and master. A pang of regret filled the *ronin* for having to meet such courage with brutal efficiency. It did not stay his sword arm, however. He sidestepped an attack and made a swift downward cut, the stroke striking the shoulder of one swordsman.

The warrior grabbed the man's sword from his insensate fingers and reversed it, drawing its length across his chest in a deep slash that severed his aorta. Zakoji's cultist dropped to the stones and moved no more. The four surviving clansmen spread apart to avoid the wounded man's fate, their blades aimed at the black-clad warrior.

The *ronin* stepped between them, a sword in each hand, like the claws of a scorpion, awaiting the next wave of attacks.

"You have a chance to live. Turn your back on Zakoji, and I shall not slay you," he told them. "You fought with courage."

The one-armed fighter lunged. The black-clad warrior blocked with one sword blade and sliced the man from hip to hip. The stroke stopped the man cold, giving the *ronin* time to sweep the other sword around to cleave the man's head cleanly from his shoulders.

He sensed the next attack, but Zakoji's fighter still managed to open up a scratch from shoulder to hip with the tip of his katana. The *ronin* reversed one sword blade and pivoted, spearing the attacker just above his kidneys. With a turn, the *ronin* grabbed the dying man's sword before he tumbled to the ground, blood leaking among the cobblestones at his feet.

And then there were two.

Two, and Zakoji.

Who knew what skills the self-proclaimed sorcerer possessed, but the *ronin* bled now. It was a scratch, but it was enough of a distraction to slow him by a heartbeat.

It could mean the difference between life and death against a man of true skill.

The two remaining swordsmen took their positions, one to his left, one to his right, but both staying in front of him, away from the water's edge.

They waited for him. Eyes searched his, sought out any sign of weakness that they could exploit. One blink, one moment of hesitation, and they would be upon him, their curved blades deep within his flesh. He gave them that blink, and as his eyes opened, he turned sideways. The two men sought the *ronin* as he faced them head-on, their goal to carve at his arms and sides as they passed him. Instead, he presented himself as a slimmer target, one sword reversed around his back, the other swooped in front of him as Zakoji's fighters passed him.

The katana he swung behind him glanced off pelvic bone as it parted its way through the side of the man who sought to harm his right side. The man on his left screamed as the black-clad swordsman's edge sunk deep into his back, lodged between two vertebrae and levered the handle from his grip. Both men fell.

The cult leader walked toward the exhausted warrior, his feet invisible beneath his robe so that he appeared to float, ghostlike. The sword cleared its scabbard with a hard push of his thumb. He leveled the point at the warrior, then down to the earth.

The *ronin* raised his sword above his head with both hands, arms pressing together in perfect position for a downward stroke. Zakoji didn't adjust his pose, still keeping his sword-point at ground level.

The *ronin* thought about the stories that Zakoji had sorcery, of sorts. He used trickery and venom to distill success in the form of a potion.

"Has your courage left you?" Zakoji chided. "Has your will to serve the emperor once again abandoned you, executioner?"

The *ronin* bristled for a moment at his old title. Each new utterance was like sand ground into an old wound. His cut ached, blood caking at the small of his back, his *hatori* grown stiff with dried blood. Sweat trickled down his forehead and neck, and each breath parted the slice in his back a little more, pain growing with each inhalation.

The *ronin* breathed deeply again. He twisted his hands around the corded handle of his blade, screwing up his strength, forcing himself back into the mind set of everything and nothing. The pain went away.

The black-clad swordsman lowered the sword from above his head and leveled the tip at Zakoji's heart.

It was with sudden fury that the cult leader lunged. The *ronin* blocked the blade with his own, sparks flew from the impact of metal on metal. The black-clad warrior tried to slip his sword past the other's defense and stab him, but only clipped the kimono sleeve, leaving a crease in the man's arm. Zakoji's blade also glanced off the *ronin*'s flesh, nicking his ribs and coming away with a trail of blood.

The cult leader lunged again, but this time the *ronin* was ready for the attack and batted it to one side. He sliced down to carve through the embroidery of the serpent on Zakoji's kimono, parting muscle and flesh as he did so. Bones gleamed from the opened wound.

The *ronin* winced as he felt his shoulder carved again. As they retreated from each other, Zakoji stumbled, teetering out of the way of a backswing that would have opened up his belly in one swoop. The *ronin*, however, felt the brutal bite of steel in flesh, his forearm nicked deeply. Blood seeped down to his grasp, both hands sticky and wet.

Zakoji snarled, clutching his wounded bosom, squeezing his kimono's slashed fabric tight against the cut. The crimson serpent image on the front darkened, growing more sinister as it drank deeply of the necromancer's blood. Wild, enraged eyes stared at the *ronin* and his control was completely gone.

Hacking with one arm, Zakoji lashed out. The *ronin* blocked two staggering blows with his sword, then pivoted out of the way. He speared the cult leader through his stomach, in the wake of a wildly missed downswing. The two fighters' bodies were tight against each other.

"You slay me now, you defeat me now…" Zakoji spit. Blood poured over his lips. "But in another lifetime…another lifetime…it is you who will taste bitterly of defeat on this very spot."

Zakoji gripped the injured *ronin*'s clothes, coughing up more blood, but in a single spasm, he was dead. The *ronin* lowered the man to the ground, shaking his head.

He stumbled away, knowing that he had to return to his infant son, to be on the road once more. He would not return this way again. He would not forget Zakoji's promise, and he offered a prayer to the universe that whoever came to this valley would be able to defeat the sorcerer's prophecy.

A convoy of two vans and two automobiles tracked its way up the side of the hill overlooking the stagnant stream. Their passing sent doves flying from tree branches, fluttering into the sky with startled warbles and the flash of wings.

A man in a black windbreaker and black jeans stared out the window at the brown water cutting its way among the cobblestones. His cold blue eyes lingered on the scene for a moment, and his memory searched, as if for some handle on the sudden wave of déjà vu that washed over him.

Mack Bolan dismissed the feeling, returning instead to his thoughts of the mission ahead.

He was posing as FBI Hostage Rescue Team Agent Matt Cooper. He popped the magazine on the Glock 23 pistol, checking the load. He reinserted it and pulled back the slide, observing the blunt .40-caliber nose of the bullet in the chamber. His stark blue eyes looked up to greet Rhode Hogan, who sat across from him in the back of the van.

"Satisfied, Agent Cooper?" Hogan asked. "I know the FBI started using those a few years ago. I wasn't sure if you'd be happy with it."

"As long as it goes bang when I pull the trigger," Bolan said, shrugging the nylon shell of his black windbreaker off his shoulders. He stuffed the gun back into its holster, with two spare magazines to balance it out.

Hogan smirked. It was all he could do to suppress a full-blown laugh. "That's the kind of attitude I like from a man. Maybe it won't be so bad having you on hand."

"I'm not exactly thrilled with this job either, Hogan."

"I know," the mercenary said. He leaned back, looking at the lush Japanese countryside. The valley dropped away as the van crawled up the road. "One man sent for this job. Usually the Feds send a dozen of you guys on one of these cases."

"One was the most we could get your boss to accept," Bolan replied. "He trusts you."

Hogan lowered his head, smiling even more widely, not looking at Bolan. "That's pretty sad, considering."

Bolan didn't make a sound, except for the noise of his palm striking the grip of his pistol.

The mercenary and his men turned on Bolan, fists and rifle butts swinging out at him.

Bolan whipped up his windbreaker and slashed it out like a whip, blinding the men on the right of him in a wave of black, snapping fabric. The movement managed to deflect a blow with one deft movement, pushing it down to snarl other attacks aimed at him.

Hogan cursed the fluid reactions of the FBI agent. While his jacket was tangling up the clubbing weapons of the men to his right, he was shouldering hard into the man on his left, his foot meeting Hogan himself in the breastbone and driving him back into his seat.

While there was strength in numbers, in the confined space of the van, there were only so many avenues of approach to attack. Bolan was shielded by the bodies of the very men who were attempting to pile on him. He swung his borrowed Glock free, but the slash of a rifle barrel forced him to aim low at Hogan's belly. He pulled the trigger on the pistol.

Nothing happened.

"Oh, by the way, the round we put in the pipe didn't have a primer. Not something you'd be able to see if you were doing a press check," Hogan said, taunting. He threw his big frame at Bolan, but again, the jumble of striking arms and weapons stopped him. Hogan's gun slammed into the Executioner's Kevlar vest and drove the wind from his lungs. With a surge, Bolan snapped his elbow into the face of the man to his left, rolling the head with the impact. He kicked at the head of the man to Hogan's right, bouncing him off the back door of the van with such ferocity that he landed in the security chief's lap.

Hands grabbed at Bolan from his right, but he had wrapped his hand around the frame of an MP-5 and he used it like an ax, chopping down on wrists and forearms. Men grunted and recoiled, hissing in pain from the slashing impacts. Hogan reached out and grasped the frame of the machine pistol, trying to twist it out of Bolan's clutches, but the Executioner brought his knee up and caught Hogan in the stomach, knocking the wind out of him. A hard shove sent the steel frame of the gun cracking into Hogan's cheek and jawline, a dizzying blow that made him see stars for a moment.

Diving low, Bolan slipped between two of Hogan's burly mercs. They had recovered from his initial attack on them, but were still slow. The warrior gave them both pause with punches to their sides, striking them in the kidneys. Choking noises exploded from their mouths and they folded to form a barrier between Hogan and his quarry.

"Stop him!" Hogan called. His beefy hand wrapped around Bolan's ankle, squeezing tight. It was like holding on to two hundred pounds of bucking bronco as the muscular form tried to rip its way to freedom. The security chief stopped the Executioner's exit from the back of the van for a moment, but the back doors had flown open during the melee, revealing the empty road behind them. Dust kicked up from the rear tires displacing gravel.

The driver called out to complain about the commotion and the sudden flapping of the rear doors in his mirrors. Bolan twisted and shoved one of the mercs hard against Hogan, their heads bouncing as the van jostled violently on the road.

With the impact of skulls, Hogan let go of Bolan's ankle, and he quickly slithered out of the back of the van.

Mack Bolan hadn't counted on Rhode Hogan to have set him up for a snatch and burn, but his skill and prowess had carried the day. When he came to a rolling halt in the middle of the road, he realized that there were still two more carloads of Hogan's mercenaries plowing up the hillside. The grille of the first chase car was only yards away from him and closing fast.

"HOW MUCH ENGLISH DO you speak?" the girl asked.

Hideaki Machida squeezed his eyes shut and fished a bottle of painkillers out of his suit's breast pocket. He shook six into his palm and popped them into his mouth, relishing the bitter chalkiness of them as he ground them with his teeth. He opened his eyes and looked at Rebecca Anthony, wishing to hell that her father's men would get here already and take her off his hands.

She was dressed all in black, including the horrendous, overdone makeup she wore around her eyes and on her lips. Machida had heard about the so-called Goth look, but he'd never read a Gothic romance novel, and doubted the heroine wore a black cable-knit sweater torn at the neck, fishnets with intentional runs in them, or piercings in one nostril, and two in the center of her lower lip.

"I asked you a question, or don't you—"

"I speak fluent English," Machida snapped. He flipped open his sunglasses and slipped them over his aching eyes before opening the rear door of the white stretch limousine and stepping out into the daylight.

"Are they—" the girl began to speak, but Machida cut her off, slamming the door and shutting out her voice.

Daimyo Botan Okudaira said the annoying girl was a part of the grand new future of their clan. The money they were getting from snatching this girl was only the beginning. Her father was a man of means, means that would give them a chance to change the entire face of Asia.

Machida shook his head. He put two and two together.

Daimyo Okudaira expected to turn the kidnapping into a gateway to link the Silver Tengu Clan and Colin Anthony's Ironcorp—a Yakuza clan with a formidable contraband distribution network hooked up to a major arms manufacturer.

Machida figured that Okudaira wanted to compete with the triads on a level they hadn't dreamed of. Machida didn't know exactly what Ironcorp produced, but it had to be important to attract Okudaira's attention in spreading his already formidable international reach.

Machida saw one of the men had out a stainless-steel Magnum revolver and was rolling the cylinder of the long, silver beast along his bronzed forearm. Unno smirked at Machida, twirled the gun and slipped it into its holster under his black vest. He shrugged his bare shoulders. His long black hair was tied off into a ponytail that swung down to midback, and when he smiled, a gold tooth glinted in the reflected sunlight. He was trying so hard to be hip and dangerous, he hurt Machida's eyes.

"Everything okay, old man?" Unno asked with that goldtoothed grin.

"Yeah. I just needed some fresh air," Machida answered, taking a few steps away from the limousine.

He looked at his team with disdain—the younger, hipper, harder Yakuza. Machida knew he was part of the old guard. The almost fifty-year old enforcer felt like he was babysitting a crew of prima-donna kids who thought they were the cutting edge.

Machida sighed, then looked at his watch.

Only a few more minutes, and he'd be done with this and back to watching his career stagnate as the head of security in Nagoya.

He looked down the road, missing the shadow of the suspended Ise Bay Highway. He was a man of the city, not the woods, but there was a quiet calm and dignity here. Machida frowned.

Thoughts of dying far from home haunted him.

MACK BOLAN HAD ESCAPED from the van with a relatively soft landing. His back hurt, but his shirt had protected him from most of the slashing, stabbing chunks of gravel in the road, and the thick, heavily toned muscles surrounding his shoulders and spine kept his bones from shattering as he somersaulted. It was not the most graceful of landings, but any one that you could walk away from, as his friend Jack Grimaldi once told him, was a great one.

The Executioner had only just come out of his roll, when he was looking at the front grille of a car bearing down on him. He had a gun with a dud round under the striker, was trying to recover his balance and heard the sound of brakes being applied behind him. Angry shouts from Rhode Hogan filled his ears.

The car screeched to a halt, the driver acting on instinct, gravel spitting from under the wheels. That was Mack Bolan's only chance, a break in the onward advance that would have crushed him. He kicked with both legs, launching himself hard out of the path of the vehicle.

More tires screeched, and there was the sound of bumpers hammering each other. Bolan didn't see the collision. He was rolling once more, this time through thick foliage at the roadside. Pliant green stalks snapped at his bare forearms and face as momentum carried him through. His shoulder felt as if it were on fire. Stinging pain and wet stickiness told him that his flesh had opened, and the enemy hadn't even fired a shot.

He tucked onto one side and used both hands on the Glock in his fist.

At least the first round in each of the magazines had

healthy looking primers. He racked the slide and ejected the dead, dud round, the next shot coming up and ready to go with one pull of the six-pound trigger. There were no safety catches or levers to be flicked into position to get the gun up and running.

The firearm was perfect for Matt Cooper, FBI agent, the smoke screen to get Mack Bolan within striking range of Yakuza daimyo Botan Okudaira.

Bolan considered his situation. This wasn't about a hostage negotiation. This wasn't about arresting someone. This was about the Executioner on the hunt for a criminal mastermind and stopping him before his organization grew strong enough to cause a turf war between Chinese and Japanese criminals—a turf war that would leave innocents dead in the cross fire and governments sweating the fallout.

The air was chilly without his jacket or a long-sleeved shirt, but it was starting to heat up as bursts of exploratory fire pumped out of the back of Hogan's van, silenced automatic fire slicing into the brush. Bolan stayed low and crabwalked toward the tree line, not afraid of getting the Glock covered in mud or dirt. The plastic-framed pistol was nearly as reliable as his Beretta in resisting mud and the elements.

Bolan moved swiftly and was far enough away that all he could make out was Hogan shouting orders, the words suppressed by distance and gunfire.

The odds didn't look good, not that Bolan was going to poke his head above the top of the foliage to expose himself. He just kept moving, walking on all fours, crouching low. His foot hit some tangled, muddy weeds and slipped. He fell to his knees and one elbow. He suppressed a grunt, but the foliage around him shook.

Bolan didn't wait for the enemy to spot and react to the sudden movement. With all his strength and speed, he launched from the foliage into the woods, ducking behind a tree just as a blast of high-velocity bullets smashed into the trunk. The Executioner swung around and contemplated returning fire, but instead held it.

Thirty-nine shots wasn't going to cut it, no matter how good a marksman he was. Not against automatic weapons with twice to three times the range of his pistol, and not against weapons in the hands of professionals who knew how to make use of every ounce of the superior shootability of a long-barreled rifle, or even a submachine gun. Bolan decided firing off even a short, discouraging burst would only attract attention and bring down the hammer of concentrated fury on him.

Instead, Bolan stayed behind the cover of a tree trunk about two feet in diameter. He was fifteen feet in from the tree line, watching for anyone starting for the woods. He watched as four men, wearing body armor and carrying big, black weapons, moved away from Hogan's convoy.

The vehicles were starting up, disappearing up the road to continue to their rendezvous with the Yakuza.

Between Bolan and the rendezvous were four heavily armed killers, better equipped and better protected than he was, and several miles of road. He looked over his hurt shoulder and saw his shirt was torn. Gravel had scraped a layer of dermis away, leaving him raw and bloodied, but the wound was superficial. His shirt flapped open at the back, and a cold wind washed over him. The weather was in the fifties, and while he knew that wouldn't be too bad for the short term, spending a whole day exposed to the cool could make him lapse into hypothermia. It happened to hikers all the time, people underdressing for the weather, thinking a spring day or a cool fall day couldn't possibly threaten their health.

Bolan gave the Glock's grip a reassuring squeeze, and

waited for the enemy gunmen to draw closer. He had cover, and he was scouting out their angles of approach.

No good, he thought. Even if he could tag one, maybe two of the mercs, the others would nail him in a cross fire. They were too well spread out, yet able to give even the farthest of their partners cover fire. If Bolan exposed himself to take down one, three more would spring into action and cut him apart.

The men stopped well before the tree line.

"Come on out, Cooper!" one of them called. "We don't want to shoot you."

Bolan checked his watch. Its surface was gouged and scratched, but the hands underneath were undisturbed. He could still make the rendezvous by cutting across country.

But first, that meant getting past the enemy.

REBECCA ANTHONY HATED her name. She'd chosen Viscious Honey as her Goth name. Her hair was the same dark golden color of honey, and nearly as slick and fluid looking. Her green eyes stared out of heavily shadowed eyelids framed with thick black.

Honey leaned against the window and sighed. She tried to remember the day before. There'd been a rave at the club, maybe just a little too much Ecstasy and then she'd been stuffed into the back of the car. A pillow case had been thrown over her head and she'd struggled, but not hard enough.

She hadn't had a chance to shower, and she had deliberately let her hair go for a while, letting natural oils and sweat darken her otherwise light and fluffy hair. Copious amounts of gel and hair spray made it glossy and heavy, spiking out and curling down in wild arcs from the center of her head. She'd colored it with grape Kool-Aid to make streaks of purple.

Her father hated her look, and that's just what she'd wanted. She didn't want to be the daughter of a millionaire who got his money from the spilled blood of the helpless, a man who helped design guidance systems for the bombs responsible for depriving people of power and water and sanitation utilities in two Gulf wars.

Honey always said she would rather be dead than living off her father's money.

She was horrified at the idea of being traded for some of that blood-spattered cash.

Honey trembled, shuddering as she realized that, because of her, the Yakuza would get hold of the kind of high-tech weaponry that would allow them to rain death on their enemies and slaughter hundreds at the touch of a button. All because she got careless and was yanked into the back of the wrong car by a group of muscle-bound Japanese thugs looking to make some extra money.

She glared at Machida.

"What was I worth to my father?" Honey asked.

"We'll learn that soon," Machida answered.

## 2

Back against the wall, outgunned and outnumbered was not a new situation for the Executioner. In fact, being outgunned and outnumbered with his back against a tree trunk wasn't even out of the ordinary. But, Bolan thought, at least he couldn't grow complacent. Not with a supersonic round smashing into the bark sending splinters of wood stinging into his biceps. He dived out of the way before a sweeping scythe of automatic weapons fire cut across the tree at chest level.

Twisting, he landed with the Glock 23's muzzle aiming at the gunman who'd taken the shot at him. Bolan pulled the trigger and there was nothing but a click. The striker had either snicked home on an empty primer, or the firing pin was malfunctioning. Or both.

Four armed men and a malfunctioning pistol would be enough to make any man give up the ghost.

But Bolan wasn't just any man.

He rolled out of the way as the machine gunner, spotting the movement on the ground, compensated. Bullets slammed into the earth where he had been only moments before. With a surge of speed, Bolan plunged himself deeper into the woods.

Bullet strikes kicked up leaves at his heels and the Executioner grimaced at the thought of having to run from a fight.

He grabbed a tree trunk and swung himself around, cutting away at a hard right angle, leaping over a log and finding himself in a clot of bushes.

He could see the men in the woods following his trail. They hadn't counted on him breaking the course so quickly. Still, each was watching the other, eyes sweeping the backs of their partners as they advanced. It was a slow leapfrog. They weren't keeping to the same pace as their prey.

Professional soldiers, to a man, and the Executioner was unarmed except for his wits, a folding knife in his pocket and the steel slide of his Glock. Wrapping his fingers around the barrel, his thumb through the trigger guard, he had a good hunk of square, exposed steel with which to smash the heavy dome of a skull, provided he had enough stealth to sneak up on these men, and had enough strength and speed to take out one man while his partner was preoccupied with advancing. The folding Applegate-Fairbairn combat knife would be his backup, four inches of deadly double-bladed steel that might be able to punch through the heavy Kevlar vests the mercs wore.

Rising silently, the Executioner advanced through the woods, circling back. He closed in on the last man in line.

Bolan sidestepped, knowing that if he missed, he was going to raise a racket. The folding dagger opened soundlessly, but locked securely. Steel in each hand, he was going to make his move, and his legs coiled up tight.

It was only four long strides, two and a leap if he timed it right, to take down the tail gunner. He took a deep, slow, silent breath, let out half and then lunged.

Gun metal struck bone head-on with a crunch, and the enemy mercenary was stunned by the unexpected impact.

Bolan dropped the knife and held on to the man, keeping him from tumbling to the ground. He was hoping the others hadn't noticed the commotion when he felt the first impacts of the 9 mm rounds strike the man that Bolan suddenly used as shield.

"He's got Tom!" came the cry, followed by a second burst.

Bolan held the back of Tom's armor. The fingers on his right hand ached from holding both the Glock and the collar of the protective vest, but his grip on the man's belt was much firmer.

A third burst hit Tom, and the multiple shocks shook the body so much that the weakened and sliced web belt came apart. The mercenary fell dead from Bolan's hands, but the Executioner still had his hands on whatever gear the gunman had on his belt.

Bullets tore through the air, and Bolan was in retreat again. He had a handgun and spare clips on the belt in his fist, and at least a mile to cross overland.

Sticking around to take out the three fully armed mercenaries would swallow too much time, allowing Hogan and the Yakuza to meet unmolested.

He couldn't let the girl exchange hands.

Bolan didn't know what would happen next, but he intended to get there before anything happened to the innocent life he was suddenly responsible for protecting.

There were no acceptable losses to the Executioner. He had only a few minutes to reach Rebecca Anthony and secure her freedom.

Bounding through the trees, the Executioner raced as fast as he could. He slowed enough to glance down at the gun he had in the holster.

He was carrying an old Walther P-38 K in his holster. With the five-inch barrel trimmed to three inches, yet still holding nine shots ready to fire with a pull of the trigger, it was an attractive weapon. Not as attractive as having fourteen rounds of bigger, fatter .40-caliber slugs, Bolan thought, but it wasn't massive missiles and having dozens of rounds of firepower that made a gun worthwhile.

It was the ability of the gunmen to hit a target.

The Executioner had that ability. And with a couple spare magazines, he figured he might actually stand a chance. It was a small chance, made even smaller as gunfire chased him through the foliage as he crossed the hillside road, but Bolan wasn't dead yet.

The Executioner charged on.

HOGAN HEARD THE CLICK of the radio and tilted it toward his mouth, his earpiece feeding him the frantic words.

"The target is climbing the hill as we speak. He's cutting across country," Frye stated on the other end.

"Damn," Hogan murmured. "He's got a useless Glock—"

"No. He got Tom."

"Christ, he's got an HK?" Hogan asked.

"No. We drove him off with automatic weapons fire, but he did manage to cut off Tom's web belt. He got that creaky old little Walther Tom loved so much," Frye explained.

Hogan took a deep breath, rolled his eyes and spoke into the radio. "Continue after Cooper. Don't let him get away. I don't need him popping up on my six when we burn the Yakuza and get the girl."

"We're in hot pursuit, sir. Unless this guy is Tarzan, there's no way he can outrace us," Frye replied.

"So why is he still alive and heading back this way when you were between him and the road?"

There was silence on the other end.

"Just as I thought," Hogan said. "I'll make sure our people are ready for him to come over the mountaintop. If you do catch him, consider your cut raised."

"Thank you, sir," Frye said.

Hogan let the radio mouthpiece rest back on his shoulder. He knew that there were more advanced designs, but the old radio was a thing of comfort, firm, solid and dependable. Just like the HK MP-5 and the Colt he had with him. Strong steel gave him a good feeling.

"Anything on their radio chatter?" Hogan asked his com man, Nickles.

"I've got nothing. There was a brief cell-phone call, but they cut it off. They're tight on their discipline," Nickles answered.

"Unless they don't have anyone to call as backup," Hogan said.

Nickles smirked. "That's thinking too positively."

"But it is an option," Hogan said. "Either way, keep watching. If they're not making calls out, then they probably have something arranged as backup."

"I'm worried about this Cooper guy," Nickles stated. "I was trying to keep track of his calls, but they were too encrypted. I couldn't get a handle on who or where he was calling."

"He's not going to be a factor. Nobody has been following us," Hogan explained. "Just keep your ears open for the Yakuza radio traffic."

"You don't think it's going to be that much of a cakewalk, do you?" Nickles asked.

"I'm carrying a shitload of firepower. Everyone on this team is. The Yakuza do not fuck around when it comes to business, and the men we're going against, they might not be military, but they are smart, tough and capable," Hogan replied. "When we make our move to get the girl, it has to be hard and it has to be fast."

Nickles smirked. "It's never soft and easy."

Hogan slapped the fore stock of his MP-5 into his meaty palm. "No, it never is."

HONEY LOOKED AT THE tree line surrounding the clearing. Only an old, overgrown path showed any alternate way off the cliff-top clearing where the Yakuza vehicles were lined up. Men spread apart, ducking into clearings and ditches, carrying high-powered rifles and handguns with them.

It was an ambush, she thought, but then she realized that would be a stupid idea. The Yakuza wanted payment for her. If they opened fire on whatever negotiators her father sent, then there was a chance that they'd damage the money or the plans. She squirmed in her seat, keeping her eyes on the path that cut up the side of the mountain.

There was a chance, she thought. She wouldn't have to go back to her father, and she could get away from these Yakuza thugs, if only she could create some kind of distraction. Her heart hammered under her breastbone, the uneasy tingle of nausea and anticipation filling her mouth with a coppery taste. She could run—

And what? Have not one but two small armies hunting her through the woods?

Anything was better than being Daddy's little hostage, she thought.

If it came to a choice between living with a murderer or dying with a bullet in her back, she'd take her chances with the slug through her spine.

Her hand touched the door release for a moment, then she looked at Machida.

"They're coming to take you home," Machida told her. "If you try to run, people will get hurt. You'll be one of them."

"Mercenaries and criminals. What's my father paying to have me freed?"

Machida shook his head. "That is not my place to say."

"I can't live with that. Because of me, some psychopath is going to get his hands on the equipment necessary to exterminate a few hundred people with the push of a button."

"We do what we have to do," Machida said. "I am bound by duty to my family to hand you over to your father's negotiators."

"No matter who suffers?" Honey asked.

Machida didn't answer, his face becoming a hard mask. She knew she'd pissed him off, and regretted it. Somewhere, deep inside, she could sense there was something different about him.

"Then, child, if you truly believe in doing your duty, I shall honor you. I will do what I have to do, and I will try to stop you, but I do not blame you for doing what you feel is the honorable thing."

"Thanks for nothing," Honey said.

The cell phone in Machida's hand rang once. He checked the readout on the caller identification. He managed a smile. "I shall be outside of the vehicle. Your father's men have just passed one of the checkpoints we've set up."

"Oh great. The cavalry is here," Honey answered. Her upper teeth clicked against the rings piercing her lower lip.

"I wish you well in your endeavor, Rebecca Anthony."

"Call me Viscious Honey," she answered.

Machida looked at her. "I wish you well, Viscious Honey."

She managed a smile as the Yakuza man left the vehicle.

NICKLES LOOKED OVER at Hogan. "There was a quick spurt of cell-phone activity. Only one ring, though."

"They're good. We must have passed a scout. For people without military-level communications equipment, they're very efficient," Hogan answered. "Any word on Cooper?"

"No sign of him since he crossed the road and went into the woods over the top of the hill."

"How long ago was that?" Hogan asked.

"Three minutes," Nickles replied.

Hogan looked at the map strapped to his forearm and judged overland travel versus the speed and distance they had traveled by road in the convoy.

"There could be a small problem," Hogan said. "This guy, Cooper, if he's a fast runner, he might actually show up on site when we're making the trade."

"One more body to add to the pile," Nickles pointed out. "He's one guy with an 8-shot pistol."

"Nine shots. Thomas always kept that thing cruiser-loaded with an extra shot in the chamber."

"Nine bullets against us?" Nickles asked. "Body armor and automatic weapons and fifteen-to-one odds."

"Not counting the Yakuza."

"Who we'll be taking care of, too."

Hogan listened to his com man's words and didn't quite believe them. There was something about the lone FBI agent. Something that wasn't right. He smelled phony as a Fed, but he actually seemed like someone Hogan would have picked up for his mercenary unit. The way he checked and cleared the Glock without even a second's sloppiness showed him as a professional weapon handler. The way he handled himself against a half-dozen men stuffed into the back of a van, and evading four armed killers in the woods was further proof that Cooper was more commando than federal cop.

Hogan knew having him pop into the scene with his gun blazing would only serve to make a tough situation even worse.

The convoy pulled slowly into the clearing.

BOLAN HAD CLEARED the top of the mountain and was three-quarters of the way to the meeting site when he slowed and evaluated his gear. The Walther P-38 K was accompanied by four magazines and a cylindrical tube. Having a sound suppressor for the little handgun would give him an element of surprise, and if he couldn't have audacity and superior firepower, he'd take stealth and deception on his side.

He quickly screwed the attachment into place and stalked slowly through the increasingly thick foliage. By the time he was in sight of the clearing, he saw Hogan's lead car arriving.

Bolan also spotted a Yakuza gunman hunkered down behind a tree trunk with a bolt-action hunting rifle. The Executioner knew it wasn't as clear-cut as a trap. Not with the kind of deal that Anthony wanted to make with the mobsters.

The sniper seemed oblivious to anything around him. Bolan knew from experience that good snipers were stealthy and could sneak in close to the enemy, but they needed a spotter, not only to confirm kills and record other intelligence, but to perform escort duty for the shooter.

Bolan was never ashamed to have someone watching his back as a sniper. But it seemed that the Yakuza gunman hadn't been given such backup.

The Executioner stayed his hand. He scanned the shrubbery, looking for other hidden forms. He stopped counting when he reached five men, all armed with hunting rifles or long-barreled revolvers with hunting scopes. He couldn't see more than the quintet present, but that was enough for him to realize that the mobsters were expecting the mercenaries to cause some trouble. The high-powered weaponry postioned at the tree line was enough to cut through even the best of body armor at that relatively short range. Firing from ambush, these five, and any others hidden at angles around the clearing, could make Hogan's mercenaries honest.

The convoy rolled to a stop as Bolan looked at the main Yakuza vehicle, a white stretch limousine parked near a small, overgrown path leading back up the mountain.

The door to the limousine opened slightly, and Bolan caught sight of a young woman's face, pale with lack of sunlight, the dark rings around her eyes highlighted by days' old makeup. Light reflected off the two metal hoops that pierced her lip. It was Rebecca Anthony, or Viscious Honey as she apparently liked to be known.

Bolan looked at the gunmen with their backs to him. He could see that the girl was looking for a distraction, and probably didn't have a clue about the armed men at the tree line who could cut her down if she tried to make a run for it. He lined up the sights of the Walther, knowing that even with a suppressor, the 9 mm bullet's flight through the trees would bounce enough supersonic echoes to make it known that he was on the scene.

He'd be giving up his advantage.

But he'd be protecting a young life.

Despite the mission to destroy the Yakuza boss, he still had a duty to protect the helpless.

MACHIDA OPENED HIS JACKET and drew a Beretta from his shoulder holster, taking a deep breath as Hogan and his men got out of the van. They approached slowly and were not subtle about their body armor and automatic weaponry. He counted them and was pleased to see that there were fifteen. Perhaps they wouldn't be foolish enough to initiate violence knowing they were outnumbered.

"Where's the girl?" Hogan called out.

"She's in the limousine. I have sharpshooters in hiding too," Machida replied quickly.

Hogan paused in his journey to meet Machida halfway. "Sharpshooters? What for?"

"To make certain you behave."

Hogan smirked.

"You come to take the girl. You will have the girl," Machida explained. "However, we will have what we need, and we will go home happy as well."

Machida watched as Hogan leaned toward one of his men.

"Oh, it's never soft and easy, huh?" Hogan whispered. "Okay, bring out the girl, and we'll give you the goods," Hogan said loudly.

The sound a walking stick disturbing the gravel path broke off the dialogue.

BOLAN LOOKED TO HIS LEFT, to the overgrown path. A gaunt man wearing old-fashioned robes was tapping a seven-foot-tall walking staff as he made his way among the rocks and weeds. His wooden sandals swept aside stones and gravel with each step. From the length of his hair and beard, he seemed to be ancient. Bolan was torn between shouting for the old man to turn back and opening fire on the marksmen in the tree line.

He glanced down and saw that even the Yakuza men were looking among themselves. They, too, wanted to say something, and one of the gunners even waved at the walker on the path. Bolan knew enough Japanese to understand the hissed "Go back!" command.

The walker stopped, gazing glassily over to the tree line, scanning it as if to catalog the men hidden among the bushes and grasses.

Bolan held his fire as the limousine door was flung open in a sudden flash of movement.

Rebecca Anthony was running for her life into the middle of a hellzone.

HOGAN SHOUTED AS HE SAW the girl break from the limousine. "She's getting away!"

Nickles ran toward the trees, making it three steps before a single gunshot into the sky brought everyone up short. Honey paused, halfway to the tree line, her feet already bleeding from cuts where the gravel of the clearing dug and jabbed into the soles of her bare feet. She was suddenly rethinking the preference of being shot in the back. She took a deep breath, then started whimpering as she glanced between Machida, Hogan and the stranger who was coming down the path.

"I'm not going to let you get away, Rebecca," Machida called out. "Everyone stays where they are."

The old man continued walking toward the tableau.

Machida switched to Japanese. "I told you, old man, stand still."

Hogan looked at the walker's eyes. They were glazed and unfocused, hard black marbles that looked everywhere and nowhere at once. It was an odd, disconcerting visage, like the world was completely beneath him. The walker didn't stop his movement, despite the command in Japanese.

"Kill him," Hogan said.

Machida regarded Hogan coldly.

BOLAN CLOSED IN ON the first sniper he'd seen, hoping to cut the distance the bullet from his Walther flew. The shorter the flight path of the bullet, the less disturbed air. The sonic crack from the 9 mm slug wouldn't draw as much attention. He glanced to his right, and saw that the snipers at the tree line were all keeping their eyes focused on Hogan's mercenaries.

Machida had just been challenged to kill the intruder on the scene, and Bolan wanted to give the old man a chance to get out of this alive.

At three feet away, Bolan stood over the gunman with the hunting rifle. The sniper sensed the Executioner's presence and swung the rifle around quickly. Bolan squeezed the trigger, and the gunman toppled lifelessly to the forest floor. Bolan's hand snagged the rifle before it clattered to the ground.

The Executioner dropped to his knees and quickly slid into the dead Yakuza soldier's place. In the shadows of the foliage around him, none of the other gunners reacted to his sudden action. The bolt-action rifle would be worth a lot in a gunfight. Ten spare rounds for the magazine were stuck into a saddle on the stock of the rifle.

The Executioner turned his attention back to the stand off in the clearing. The walker passed by Rebecca Anthony as she stood in the middle of the gravel. The spindly figure stopped, looking her over.

"Dammit... I just want to get away from all of this," she said, voice trembling and soft, but full of angry resolve.

Bolan shouldered the hunting rifle. He'd have five, maybe six shots before he had to reload or switch to the Walther, but he refused to let the girl be harmed.

The walker grabbed her wrist and sneered, flipping aside his robes.

That's when everything that Bolan knew about the situation turned upside down. The old man was suddenly sporting a fistful of Uzi.

**3**

When the walker pulled out his gun and yanked the girl in close to his body, several things happened at once.

The fleeing hostage screamed in terror. Her black-lipstick-smeared mouth opened wide, and she clutched a wiry arm of the walker.

The Yakuza head soldier, leveled one Beretta at Hogan and quickly drew a second pistol to aim at the walker. He shouted for his men to remain calm, but even from where he sat, Bolan could see that there was a tremor as he aimed unsteadily at the old man with the Uzi.

Hogan shouldered his MP-5, ready to spray either the Yakuza leader or the stranger who'd grabbed the girl. His bulletlike head lowered over the sights, deep-set eyes squinting.

The Executioner tightened his grip on the hunting rifle in his hands, brain racing to evaluate which was the greatest threat to the hostage.

The walker laughed as he pressed the Uzi to the girl's temple. She closed her mouth but still looked around, the muzzle sliding all over her greasy, slicked hair.

Bolan couldn't risk a head shot on the goon, in case he pulled the trigger on the girl. He swept the meeting ground. Mercenaries and mobsters alike were taking cover behind vehicles, and to either side of him, along the tree line, gunmen were communicating from their hiding spots. Everyone was trying to figure out what to do.

"Kojo," someone said. A trail of Japanese followed that was too quick for Bolan to understand, but he knew it was directed at him.

"*Hai,*" Bolan whispered in response. He hoped to hell he hadn't blown it.

There was a sudden movement to his left. A harsh sentence was uttered, and Bolan brought up his Walther, pumping out a single bullet into the darkness. The 9 mm slug quietly hit its target, but the gunman gave a scream as he tumbled from the tree line.

The walker spun, and the Uzi came away from the girl's head. The dying Yakuza shooter crashed into a clump of tall grass, and the old man twisted, looking around for more enemies in the trees.

The Goth girl seized the opportunity, bent double and broke away from the man. She charged madly toward the path, paying no heed to the sharp stones digging into her feet. Fear drove her onward.

Bolan shouldered his rifle, targeting Hogan, who was in midswing to shoot down the Anthony girl. Bolan squeezed the trigger. He felt the hot splash of a stray shotgun pellet slice across his shoulder midshot. The Executioner's round was off target.

Machida blasted the walker full in the chest with his Beretta, while others opened up on the man, throwing him to the ground.

Hogan grunted, his weapon getting off two shots, then stopping short as a .30-caliber rifle bullet smashed into the frame of his machine pistol and drove him onto his back. Bolan adjusted his aim and threw the bolt on the rifle, hurriedly chambering another shot.

"Hogan! There's someone else in the tree line!" Machida warned. The gangster opened fire with his other Beretta. The Yakuza men swung their weapons to open fire on the Executioner's position, but by that time, Bolan was already hot-footing it out of the way.

The mercenaries held their fire, looking on in disbelief as the Japanese mobsters ignored them, turning their attention on some mystery threat.

"Dammit! Shoot the trees!" Hogan roared at his men. He was aching from being slammed in the chest by his own gun. His hand hurt, but he pulled his Colt and opened fire on the spot where the single rifle shot had come from.

THE EXECUTIONER CHARGED through the woods, heading in the direction of the path where Rebecca Anthony intended to make her escape. While on the run, he threw the bolt on the hunting rifle to chamber another round and fired into the shadowed mass of a gunman blazing away with his handgun. The shooter screamed, and his body tumbled away. The number of bullets slicing through the forest hadn't decreased; they were still out for his blood. Bolan cut hard to the right, charging to where he estimated the young woman would be on the path.

HONEY'S FEET HURT as she made the run along the path. She expected one of the bullets behind her to thunder into her flesh and drop her any minute. She felt completely helpless as she pumped her legs, striving to survive for just a few more yards, to get around the bend and into the foliage.

The prospect of getting shot while escaping filled her with dread. The plan to run for her life and strike out for her freedom seemed like the scatterbrained plot of a woman doomed to die.

Then two hundred pounds of muscle rammed into her in a blindsiding crash. One strong arm scooped her off her cut and bloody feet and carried her into the heavy bushes and trees on the opposite side of the path, as gunfire crackled all around.

"Stop shooting! Stop shooting! He has the girl!" Machida shouted.

"Fuck!" Hogan screamed. "Get into the woods!"

Honey stared up at the man carrying her. He was craggy faced, and intense. However, the way he held her, putting both arms around her to support her, told her something.

This black-haired stranger had no business with either the Yakuza or the mercenaries who showed up to retrieve her for her father.

THE WALKER STIRRED. He sat up with a sudden lurch and aimed at Machida, holding down the trigger of his Uzi. Despite a blood-spattered face, the slender old man was still in fighting form, and if the Yakuza boss hadn't spotted the motion out of the corner of his eye, he would have been cut down where he stood. As it was, the limousine was peppered with 9 mm holes.

Hogan swung around the back of the car and pulled the trigger on his Colt .45, snapping two shots into the head of the walker, blowing off a huge chunk of skull in the process.

This time, the Uzi-toting old man slumped for good.

Machida and Hogan walked slowly to the lifeless man. Both reloaded their pistols on the slow, uncertain journey over, and saw that the wisps of mustache and beard were glued-on fakes, half-washed away by the spray of blood from the first salvo of fire the combined forces launched at him.

Machida bent and pulled at the ratty gray robes of the old man and saw the black Kevlar armor underneath. "What the hell is this?" he asked.

"You tell me, Hoss," Hogan said. He raised and leveled his Colt at the Japanese mobster. Machida looked at him but kept his pistol aimed at the ground.

"You think I wanted this fool to let the girl get away?" Machida asked. "She's running into the woods."

"This is your country, man. You had men in the tree line," Hogan grumbled.

Machida shook his head. "We'll help you find the girl. Under one condition."

"You're giving me new conditions for the deal? You already have the ransom from Anthony."

"I'm not talking about the blueprints," Machida answered. "Well, in a way I am."

Hogan lowered his gun. "What are you talking about, then?"

"You came dressed to kill, so to speak. That's why I had men watching, ready to burn you back. I figured you'd have body armor and automatic weapons," Machida answered. "What I didn't anticipate were the two problems coming out of the woods."

"And how do you know they were two separate problems?"

"Simple. One didn't want his presence known, but his hand was forced when you were about to shoot the girl," Machida answered. "This one is Japanese. I'm not sure about the identity of the other man...."

"He's allegedly an FBI agent named Matt Cooper," Hogan replied.

"Allegedly an FBI agent? Or allegedly named Matt Cooper?" Machida inquired further.

"Both. I'm thinking he was using us to get closer to you and your boss, and just ended up on the wrong end of our sting," Hogan answered.

Machida rubbed his chin. "A temporary truce, then? It'll be more profitable to work together. And there is nothing wrong with taking the blueprints you have, and making two copies of them. One you can blackmail Anthony with, and one we can sell on the black market."

Hogan tilted his head. "It sounds like a win-win situation."

"But does it sound acceptable to you?"

The mercenary put his hand forth. "It's a deal."

Machida didn't trust the American as they pressed flesh, but at least it would give the Yakuza headman some stretch to figure out how to deal with him.

BOLAN CAME TO A HALT, his reserves of strength exhausted during his frantic run through the trees with Rebecca Honey in his arms. He set her down and squatted, looking at her feet.

"What're you stopping here for?" Honey asked, trying to mask her doubt and uncertainty with a hard edge to her voice.

Bolan didn't bother looking up from the cuts on the soles of her feet. Most of them were shallow, but a couple of them were deep and painful looking, seeping blood. He grabbed his T-shirt and ripped it. There was a slight gasp as Honey looked at his naked abdomen.

"Did you lose a fight with a weed cutter?" she asked.

Bolan shook his head. "Occupational hazard. Scar tissue. Your feet look like they'll be okay if I can control the bleeding with some direct pressure compresses."

"And all you have is your T-shirt. What happened, you forgot to go to the standard action-hero supermarket before going on this little adventure?" Honey asked. She looked down at herself, her deliberately torn clothing had no extra material to add to her own healing.

"Why the hell were my father's men trying to shoot me?"

"They wanted more money," Bolan answered.

"And you?"

"Name's Matt Cooper. FBI Hostage Rescue Team. Rebecca…"

"Call me Viscious Honey…or Honey for short."

Bolan looked at her. "Honey, we're cut off and have to find some transportation out of this valley. There are men hunting us down who would like nothing better than to gut me like a fish and leave me to watch whatever they're going to do to you."

Honey nodded. "Let 'em try something. I'll make it cost them. Though, I am curious at how well the kidnappers treated me."

"Not due to honor. Just smart business on the part of the Yakuza. However, Hogan's going to show you off, roughed up, probably even tape any beating or other abuse they inflict on you," Bolan said.

"I'm not going back to my father."

Bolan sighed. "I don't care what you do. I just want to make sure you're away and safe. If you do what I say, things will be all right."

Bolan tightened the strip of cloth around Honey's foot and she gasped again, wincing in pain. Her foot was wrapped from the ball to near the ankle, a single restraining strap up around her ankle providing her with some security for her injured foot. Bolan pressed his thumb along her other foot, but only received a faint hiss as he touched one particularly deep cut.

"I'm trying to give the worst, most painful cuts as much protection as I can. I wish there was a better way, but at least your injuries will be wrapped up until I can get you some footwear," Bolan said. "If we're lucky, the next Yakuza guy I fight will have boots you can manage in."

Honey smirked. "Great. You're not only a shining knight, you're an eternal optimist."

"Planning ahead for possibilities and probabilities. I'm hoping to avoid conflict the rest of the way back to Tokyo, but in case we can't, I'm going to make the most of the fights," Bolan answered. "Even if that means looting a few dead bodies."

Honey's lip quivered, then she shrugged. "I don't mind. They kidnapped me, and they want to kidnap me again."

Bolan took a moment to withdraw the Walther and replace its partially spent magazine with a fresh one. He set the weapon in the grass and Honey reached for it. Bolan froze, looking at her as she held the weapon in her lap.

"I don't want to leave it behind," she said. "It's the only gun you have, right?"

Bolan regretted ditching the hunting rifle, but he had no spare ammunition for it, and he'd needed his arms free to carry Honey. "Yeah."

Bolan removed the Yakuza gun belt and unhooked the pouches and holster from it. They were all connected to the belt, by J-hooks, so he didn't have to take off his own belt and run it through the loops. He clipped them on firmly, then stashed the partially spent magazine in its pouch. He held out his hand for the Walther.

Honey seemed reluctant to turn it over, though she wasn't aiming it at him.

"Honey, we don't have time for this. What's wrong?"

"How do I know I can trust you?" she asked. "You don't look like an FBI agent."

"What makes you think that?" Bolan asked.

Honey pointed to the scars across his body, visible through the open front of his torn shirt. "An FBI agent with that much scar tissue would have had a desk job by now. Knifed and shot that many times? Plus you have another gun," she said, pointing at his shoulder.

Bolan gingerly slid out of the Glock's holster, the leather scraping his injury.

"Hogan, your father's mercenary, gave me a dead pistol. Took the firing pin out so it wouldn't shoot. I had to ditch it."

He took the shoulder holster and began digging briefly. When he had a hole big enough, he shoved the useless belt, holster and Glock ammunition into it then pushed and smoothed leaves and dirt back over it.

Honey moved closer to Bolan, her eyes wide. She handed over the Walther, and Bolan took it, instinctively knowing that their pursuers were close. He made a count of the enemy. There were nine visible across the section of woods that he could see.

"That way," Bolan said, pointing. "I'll be right behind you."

"Yeah. Let me go first into any traps?" Honey asked. "Who knows what kind of shit that creepy skinny guy left all over this valley."

"Don't make any noise," Bolan answered. "They've slowed down, and they're looking for tracks."

Honey glanced back at the trail Bolan's big boots had dug up in his desperate run. She looked to him, doubtful, but he nodded her on. She turned and scrambled along as fast as she could without making the leaves rustle loudly with her passing. Behind her, Bolan followed, using a branch to wipe out their tracks.

They moved slow and low, and they kept their heads below the level of the saplings and tall grasses growing between the trees.

On the other side of some waist-high grasses, Honey paused. Bolan slipped in beside her.

"Aww, dammit. We're closing in on a rise," she noted. "They'll see us."

"Cut right. We'll travel parallel to them. The ground is uneven and there's a depression at the base of those trees," Bolan whispered. "Get moving."

TOSHIEE RAN ACROSS the compound. He knew that Master Zakoji was not to be interrupted, but with the sounds of gunfire rattling on the hill overhead, there was a threat of their facility being discovered.

Camouflage netting cast crazy, obscene shadows on the ground as he raced across the camp to the main building, where Zakoji kept his laboratory and office. It was wide and squat, and he knew that it sunk deep into the ground, where the bodies were taken, to be changed by the almost sorcerous machinations of Master Zakoji's whitecoats.

Toshiee threw open the doors in time to see his leader, the man chosen by God to carry on the name of the great alchemist who dared defy a corrupt shogun, reborn in this time to bring Japan back to glory. He clapped his fist to his chest and bowed swiftly.

"What is it?" Zakoji asked, puffing a cigarette as he overlooked the glass enclosed underground labs.

"There was the sound of gunfire on the hill," Toshiee said breathlessly.

"The Yakuza bring another of their victims and execute him, and you worry about that?"

"There was much gunfire," Toshiee continued. "More than just when they render a body useless to you, my lord. This was the sound of thunder splitting the air. Like the sounds of a great battle."

Zakoji turned, narrowing his gaze. He then nodded to the man to his left. "See if our scout on the hill is responding."

"Great Master, so soon on the heels of the previous intrusion—"

"I shall have to get in touch with our men dealing with him," Zakoji said. "You have done well."

The young man bowed again. He caught the flurry of robes as his master turned, glimpsed the twisting form of the great crimson serpent embroidered into his kimono as he disappeared up the stairs toward his office.

TOJU SAKEI, KNOWN TO his followers as Master Zakoji, tore through the door to his office, his mind racing.

It couldn't have been coincidence that brought a gun battle to his doorstep so soon after the government agent invaded. And yet, why would federal agents begin a gun battle so close by, ruining their element of surprise?

Sakei shook the many possibilities out of his mind. He needed all the information he could get. He glanced over to Umon, one of his lieutenants.

"Any word from our sentry?"

"Kawai isn't answering his radio," Umon answered, bowing his head reverently.

"Call our team torturing the government man back to the compound. And send some patrols into the woods. I want everyone on full alert, that means body armor and automatic weapons," Sakei said.

"Who do you think is attacking us?" another man, Rikyu, asked.

"I'm not sure we are being attacked," Sakei responded. He rubbed his black-bristled chin. "I think someone else brought their fight with the Yakuza into our backyard."

Umon and Rikyu glanced at each other. "And if the Yakuza discover that the men they've been burying over the years are missing?" Umon asked.

"We won't let them live long enough to analyze that information," Sakei assured them. "Send out the patrols. Shoot to kill!"

Umon and Rikyu vacated his office, and Sakei looked out over the compound.

If he was going to take over Japan, fulfilling the legacy of the original Master Zakoji, he was going to need a few more days of privacy. Once he perfected the disease's interactions with the corpses, then he would be able to bring down the great gleaming cities of steel and glass, sweeping away the neon modernization that poisoned the beautiful nation he lived in. He could make Japan a simpler, more noble land once again.

It was regrettable that he had to use the trappings of modern science, but the germ, the lowliest of all organisms, was older than mankind. It was ancient, and thus, in a way, it was worthy of his goal. Did not the alchemist Zakoji develop superior poisons and diseases with which to strike down his enemies centuries ago?

All that came to an end when the lone swordsman came to the secluded valley. Zakoji's dying curse against the man had been heard over and over again, in tale upon tale in Sakei's family.

Sakei thought that the government agent being tortured to death on the hill might be the reincarnation of that lone swordsman.

But Sakei knew that the sounds of battle so soon after sending the Koancho agent off to die was a sign. He hadn't destroyed the reincarnation of the man in black.

But he would soon get his chance.

**4**

The Executioner continued to obliterate their back trail with the branch, taking care not to bob his head into view as he watched the pursuing team of Yakuza gunmen and American mercenaries. The enemy was hot on their trail to retrieve the young woman, and he had only a single 9 mm pistol with a short barrel and an 8-shot magazine. There was a real danger of Honey Anthony being gunned down alongside him as he tried to protect her.

The girl was keeping her cool, despite the bandages swathed around her bare feet and the fact that she was crawling literally on the ground. Occasionally she'd give a grunt of effort as she moved a limb and found herself overstrained in her position. Fear kept her head down, though. Fear and tenacity.

Bolan knew from reports that she was hardly fighting material, but she clearly had courage.

Bolan knew he could have been worse off, but even so, this wasn't a good situation. He desperately wanted to get hold of a larger weapon, like an M-16, something that had the necessary punch to knock out large groups of enemies.

As it was, he was left with his best weapon. His mind.

Honey stopped abruptly, and Bolan dropped to one knee, checking on their pursuers. They were still about fifty yards behind in the forest, barely visible. He glanced at the girl. She was staring at the top of a hill up ahead.

"More bad guys?" she whispered.

Bolan took in the scene. A man was jammed into a tree, and three men with knives stood around him. His shirt was a gory mess, and his face a crimson mask of dried blood. The trio was laughing as it was doing its ghastly butcher's work. Bolan frowned.

"They might be with that man who grabbed you back in the clearing," Bolan noted.

Honey looked at him. "You think?"

The Executioner almost smirked. "If I can get the jump on them, I might be able to pick up some spare firepower."

"That would be a good thing," Honey said. The prospect of violence played across her face with a displeasure that Bolan knew all too well. It mirrored his own feelings. Violence was the last resort, but in Bolan's world, he was already called in when that point had been looted, pillaged and burned to the ground.

"Stay close behind me," Bolan whispered. He dropped his branch and swung around, making his way up the side of the rise. He looked back and saw that no one had spotted the outlines of the two black-clad people as they climbed toward the quartet near the killing tree.

As they closed in, the coppery smell of blood threatened to make Honey gag. She held it down, though. Bolan was inured to such scents.

He drew his Walther from its holster and leveled the front sight at the man nearest the victim pinned on the tree. The tortured man looked up, his dark eyes glassy, his face blood-spattered, but he didn't give away the Executioner's presence.

A single shot puffed out from the Walther. It smashed into the back of the first torturer's head and blew open the skull.

Chunks of brain matter and blood rained in a halo around the knife-wielding maniac before his body tumbled to the ground.

The other two men spun. One was in the middle of lighting his cigarette, a machete tucked under one armpit. The other man glanced at the weapons they had rested against the side of a log, stocks in the dirt, barrels pointing into the sky.

Bolan swung the Walther at the gunman who was looking at the guns. A bullet crossed the distance between them before he could dive and scoop up a sawed-off shotgun resting against the fallen tree trunk. It struck the gunman just above his clavicle, and tore out a messy chunk of throat. Blood exploded from the shotgunner's mouth and he collapsed against the line of weapons, his body covering them.

Bolan turned his attention to the machete-wielding cigarette smoker. He'd abandoned his efforts to light his smoke and brought his blade out from under his armpit in a single, fluid movement. The tip of the blade connected with the end of the Walther's sound suppressor after a rapid lunge and redirected the next 9 mm slug into the sky.

The Executioner let the Walther swing to the wayside and freed his left hand from its support position in his shooting grip. He speared the machete-wielding torturer in the stomach with a swift punch, then slammed the steel frame of the Walther hard against the sadist's cheek. Skin split and bone cracked under the powerful impact, and the man fell backward, stunned.

Bolan swept his leg around and hooked the man's ankle. Another hard left hand snapped into the killer's chest with a hollow thump, and the man tumbled, crashing to the forest floor. The machete man snarled and kicked Bolan hard in the knee before the Executioner could aim his Walther at the downed man. A 9mm bullet dug up dirt and leaves next to the blademan's head before Bolan fell to the ground next to his foe.

The man swung his machete around, but Bolan caught his wrist, squeezing hard to grind the forearm bones and wrist cartilage together. The Japanese man screamed and let go of the blade. Bolan lurched to one knee and rapped the killer hard across the jaw with the butt of his pistol. Bone crunched on impact, and the blademan went still.

The Executioner panted, the brief battle accentuating the amount of energy he'd burned in the past half hour without rest. The relentless pace was draining his reserves of strength. He glanced over Honey. "Check their shoe sizes against yours."

Honey gawked at him. "You're shitting me, right?"

"You need to protect your feet, so just put some shoes on."

Honey glared at Bolan, then bent to get the shoes.

He got up, took an M-16-like rifle and walked over to the man on the tree.

"Can you speak English?" Bolan asked in his halting Japanese.

"*Hai*, a little," the wounded man said. His voice came out as a hoarse croak, and his eyes were heavily lidded.

"What's going on here?" Bolan asked. "Who were these men?"

"These are the men of the Burakku Uwibami Clan. They are a cult—" He coughed up some blood. "I appear to be dying…"

Bolan took his knife out and cut the man's bonds. "You're not going to die."

The man looked him over and smiled. He slumped against Bolan, his blood spattering across the Executioner's clothes.

"Who are you?" Bolan asked.

"My name is Chiba. I am with Koancho."

Bolan nodded. The Japanese Public Security Investigation Agency was a top secret counterintelligence agency. Very little was known about them, but they handled investigations both inside and outside of the country. If Koancho was involved, Bolan knew, the cult clan was a possible world-class threat.

Chiba continued. "The cult…has been developing a new germ warfare weapon. If it succeeds…"

He coughed again, there was a rattling sound in his chest. "You must stop Zakoji."

Bolan looked down the hill. He, Chiba and Honey were behind the tree and out of sight of the Yakuza and mercenaries hunting them, but it wouldn't take long for them to come up the hill.

"Zakoji claims that his ancestor was first defeated by an executioner in black. He claimed that someday, they would meet again, and the blood of that executioner's reincarnation would redden the ground at his feet…"

Chiba's eyes glazed over. "That is why he was bleeding me… He thought… I was… the executioner…"

The Koancho agent's lips stilled, his eyes staring sightlessly from a lifeless face. Stunned, Bolan closed Chiba's eyelids and laid him on the ground.

"Why was he talking about executioners?" Honey asked.

Bolan didn't say a word.

The flash of a laser sight suddenly crossed his shoulder.

HOGAN PAUSED, holding his receiver a little tighter.

"This is Higgins. We've got activity at the tree line. There seems to be more than just Cooper in these woods," the mercenary said.

"Are they together or what?" Hogan asked.

"Seemed like there was a scuffle at the top of the ridge. I'm not sure, but maybe silenced gunfire."

"Take out Cooper, but don't harm the girl. If she bolts, put a bullet in her arm or leg. Nothing fatal," Hogan ordered.

He looked at Machida, who stared on, his face unreadable. "Do you have a problem with shooting the girl?" Hogan asked.

"It does not matter. I am not on the scene to take the shot," Machida replied.

"Nobody likes a smart-ass," Hogan grumbled.

"I will keep that in mind."

Hogan was about to growl when he saw movement out of the corner of his eye. Branches shifted slightly, but not in the direction of the breeze. He turned and swung up his spare machine pistol. "Indian country!"

The mercenaries around him understood the two-word shorthand for ambush. The Yakuza gunmen in the clearing with them needed only to see Hogan's people dive for cover to react. Machida's and Hogan's forces crouched, aiming outward around the clearing.

Hogan directed the first gunfire. He blasted away with a borrowed machine pistol and swept the area of tree line that had moved out of sync. A gunman grunted and stumbled into view, but he wasn't killed by the initial blast. The ambusher's weapon spoke, chopping off a mercenary at the knees, then walked a blast of gunfire up into the stomach of a Yakuza gunman.

The raider's victory was short-lived, however. Mercenary and mobster alike lit him up with their weaponry, focusing the arc of their fire on the woods around him in a blasting firestorm of activity. Hogan ducked behind the limousine as more incoming gunfire chopped its side panels apart. Machida was right at Hogan's heels, returning fire with his two Berettas even though he couldn't see anything.

"Cease-fire! Cease-fire!" Hogan called out.

Mercenaries and Yakuza gunmen dragged their injured and dying companions to cover behind the parked convoy of vehicles in the clearing. Moans of the wounded resonated to drown out the ringing in Hogan's ears that resulted from the firestorm of automatic weapons cutting the air.

Hogan reloaded his weapon and looked around. He didn't dare call out to confirm the condition of his men. Betraying the status of their remaining forces would leave them open for any attackers to move in and finish them off. He didn't know how many were striking from the woods, but he wasn't going down so easily.

Machida was reloading his two pistols. "It seems the old man had friends in this area," he said softly. "And they are well-armed."

"No kidding," Hogan snarled. "Is there a reason for you to tell me the obvious?"

"It is a more productive use of nervous energy than screaming in fear," the Yakuza man replied. He stuffed one Beretta into its holster, keeping the other out. His free hand dived immediately for his cell phone, and he hit the speed dial.

"What are you doing?" Hogan asked.

"I am calling for my backup. You call for yours. We're not leaving without our intended trade," Machida answered. "Or else."

"Or else what?"

Machida's silent stare was more effective than any boast. His calm face housed eyes full of black clouds of fury.

There were no empty threats coming from this man.

BOLAN HIT THE GROUND, bullets passing so close above him he could feel the whipcracks of their path through the air. He rolled out from behind the log and looked down at the assembly of men taking cover among the trees.

Honey busied herself, pulling guns from underneath the body of one of their dead enemies. She tried not to look at the bloodied corpse of Chiba.

Bolan shouldered the M-16 and pulled the trigger. His first shot was a miss, hitting a tree trunk instead of an armed mercenary. The merc ducked behind cover as the single 5.56 mm round smashed into the tree and splinters sprayed.

The Executioner adjusted his aim. He'd hoped that the sights were centered for his eyes, but they were a few inches off. When he got a chance, he'd have to adjust the sights more to his point of aim. For the moment, he faked it with windage and popped off another shot that took a Yakuza man in the shoulder. The rifle round tore into bone and flesh, and exited the mobster's body in a shattering explosion of stringy pulp. The man howled and spun to the ground.

Another armed gunman swung around a tree and received a shot through the stomach. He folded over and Bolan punched a second shot into his exposed neck, leaving him with a shattered spine and a cored heart.

The Executioner was out of time. He rolled back swiftly as bullets stormed against the log. The drumbeat of multiple rounds filled the air, and Honey curled up tight, clutching two guns to her chest.

There was a lull in the shooting below, and Bolan waited, knowing he would have the opportunity to whittle the enemy odds further.

The Executioner poked around the corner of the log and saw a pair of mercenaries break off from the group. He snap aimed at them, following their black silhouettes as they cut through the green foliage. They were close together, and Bolan knew they were being sloppy with haste. He fired a single bullet into the merc at the rear of the two-man procession and knocked him sideways. The other gunman whirled to catch a stitching duet of slugs across his chest.

The black-clad mercenary stumbled for a moment, then staggered into a shooting position. Bolan had hit the man square in his body armor, and it had held. The Executioner adjusted his aim and fired at the gunner's head. It took three pulls of the trigger before he was rewarded with a reaction, the jerk of the body and the spitting mist of crimson. The enemy rifleman flopped onto his back.

A wall of lead hammered into the log and the dirt around them, chunks of sod and leaves raining down all over them.

"Did they have any spare magazines?" Bolan asked.

Honey, adjusting the pair of deadman's loafers, paused to glare at him. "I found shotgun shells in one guy's pocket. And one of these things."

She held up an Uzi magazine.

It wasn't going to do much against men with body armor. The M-16 carbine was going to have to last him until he could get something with armor-piercing ammunition.

A hollow thump sounded from down below, and Bolan's stomach lurched.

The 40 mm grenade smashed into the ground near the log and the shock wave forced the rifle from Bolan's fingers, even as the three-foot trunk protected him from the bulk of the blast. Honey screamed and folded in two at the sound of the eruption, but Bolan, despite sore and raw-skinned fingers and palms, snatched for the Uzi she was clutching. She immediately grabbed a shot gun.

The Executioner took her hand and pulled her away from the fallen trunk.

"But…" she began.

"Move!" Bolan ordered. He watched her feet as they ran. They were lucky that one of the men Bolan had shot had small feet. The bandages helped fill out the slightly wobbly shoes she wore. They were going to need every bit of sure footedness to make it down the hill on the other side and cut into the much thicker forest.

Bolan knew he could only count on the mercenaries and mobsters to delay for a few minutes. They would make a cautious climb up the hill, covering one another to avoid being drawn into an ambush.

He'd given them something to think about by bringing down three of them. It was a third of the number he'd counted, but someone had his hands on some serious firepower. Only the luncky presence of a huge log had prevented injury to Honey and himself. Bolan calculated that an M-16 was most likely the offending tool.

He assessed the odds. The Uzi was a formidable weapon, but it didn't have the range or penetration of the M-16 part of the combo. And nothing matched the devastation of a 40 mm grenade.

The only thing the Executioner had was his marksmanship. If he and Honey could hide, if they could get into a good sniper's roost to pick off their enemies with the Uzi, then he could take out the grenadier first.

Outgunned. Outmanned. On the run with an untrained ingenue in tow.

Still, it was nothing new. He hadn't been this behind the eight ball in a while, but Bolan hated being on the defensive.

He also had the death cult to think about. The Burakku Uwibami clan was familiar to the Executioner. As part and parcel of his job, he constantly read about and kept abreast of dangerous organizations around the world. Also known among western intelligence agencies by its translated name, the Black Serpents, it was run by a man who called himself Zakoji, after a sixteenth century alchemist who sought to tear down the shogunate.

It was thought that the cult may have had connections to Tokyo subway nerve gas attack of the late nineties. It was known to deal with suppliers of weapons of mass destruction in order to achieve its ultimate goal of rendering the cities of Japan useless.

Then the clan could return the nation to a simpler time.

Bolan could hardly believe that he'd managed to stumble into not one but three separate plots on one mission. The Yakuza and the mercenaries both seemed to want to use the blueprints designed by Honey's father to sell on the black market to ready and willing buyers. He could only hope that Hogan and Machida would weaken themselves with infighting, and figured that his prospects were good in that regard. Both sides knew that to allow another to have the plans would make its own less valuable. Potential buyers would be able to comparison shop between the two groups, forcing the costs down to ridiculously low levels.

He knew the truce between the mercenaries and the Yakuza would only be temporary, one that would last only as long as it took for them to find the girl and kill Bolan.

"Cooper," Honey spoke up as they slowed down. "Where next? I mean, we're in the middle of some serious shit."

"I can't let you fall back into their hands," Bolan told Honey.

"But what about this guy…Zakoji? Chiba said he was bad news."

Bolan realized that time was runnig out. Zakoji and the Black Serpent clan wouldn't stick around long, not after having Chiba show up on their doorstep, and then to have two groups of raiders stumble onto their hiding place. No matter what ancient traditions the cult held, they wouldn't be foolish enough to stay in a place that suddenly turned out to be busier than Grand Central Station.

"There's a small gully emptying out down that way." Bolan pointed. "It'll give us some protection out of sight from anyone on the hill, and we might even be able to cut across the valley before they spot it."

"You spotted it," Honey pointed out.

"We'll have a head start. How are your feet?"

Honey flexed her feet in the loafers. "They're not my usual combat boots, but for a dead guy's kicks, they're pretty comfortable."

"Stay by my side," Bolan said. "I'm not bothering with covering our back trail this time."

"Why not?" Honey asked.

"Too much chance of you running into an ambush by Zakoji's people. I want to be on hand to protect you," he said. "You have the magazine for the Uzi?"

She handed it over, a little reluctantly.

"Listen, Honey," Bolan told her. "I know you think violence is abhorrent, but believe it or not so do I. The only trouble is our opponents don't."

"I know. I know that you have to fight," she answered. She glanced back. "Normally death and gloom are stuff I like, but not with real blood and brains and guts all over the place."

"They're stone-cold killers," Bolan replied. "The only reason you weren't hurt was because then you wouldn't be worth a tenth of what your father is risking to get you back."

Honey nodded. Her eyes clouded over, and she gripped the shotgun tighter.

"What are you going to do with that?" Bolan asked her.

"I'm not sure yet," Honey said.

"Then you don't have any business carrying a firearm." He walked with her quickly, moving down the gully at the base of the hill. Overhead, the treetops cut off any view of the hilltop, but he could hear the sound of voices up above. He didn't want to distract himself debating with her.

"It makes me feel better knowing I have a way out," Honey said in a desperate whisper.

"I'm not going to let them take you," Bolan replied, keeping his voice low.

Honey shook her head. "I know, but I want to at least…at least have an option."

She clutched the shotgun tighter, keeping her hands away from the trigger.

"Let me make sure it's safe, then," Bolan told her. "I'll give it right back."

He slung the Uzi and did a quick manual check on the shotgun. There was no round in the chamber, but a thumb-press told him that the magazine tube, long enough for four shots, was full to capacity. "Okay, this is safe enough that it won't accidentally go off if you trip and fall. If it comes time to shoot, though, pull the slide and hold on tight with both hands."

Honey nodded, looking at the weapon a little nervously. Then she clutched it, gripping it tightly, like a cherished toy.

Bolan hoped that it wouldn't come to involving her in a firefight.

**5**

Sakei grimaced at the news.

All communications had been lost with the men who were interrogating the Koancho agent.

His team sent to the clearing where the gunfire occurred had encountered a far smaller force than was expected. However, they had taken casualties, despite their body armor and the element of surprise.

And worse, the force in the clearing had punched out, escaping through the woods and into the forest.

It was enough to make him wish that his clan were really made of evil, magical serpents. Maybe the power of ancient sorcery combined with awesome reptilian power would be enough to wipe the scourge of these invaders from his valley. This was where his family had been nurturing the Burakku Uwibami across the centuries, and nothing short of death would drive him from this land.

He contemplated using some of the weapons he'd acquired from the Syrians to clear out the enemy. After all, his people were issued with atropine injectors to protect them from the effects of nerve gas. He doubted anyone who arranged a meeting in the wrong place at the wrong time would have had the forethought to come prepared for tabun or sarin gases.

"Zakoji, the team we sent to the hilltop is reporting in

early. They've heard grenade detonations," one of his men said, interrupting his thoughts. "This is getting worse and worse."

"They're giving away their capabilities. Have our people encountered the intruders yet?" Sakei asked.

"No," the man replied. "They're still on approach."

"Do not engage the enemy unless we're certain of a victory. We underestimated them up on the cliff, and we took losses without measurable success," Sakei answered. "Tell them to shadow the intruders, and when they get the chance, take out the heaviest firepower first."

"Yes. It is as you wish."

The lieutenant spun on one heel and left the command center. The other men were busy monitoring communications and the security sensors networked all across the forest. According to their readings, there were more than two dozen men running around.

Of particular note were two figures who kept away from one of the larger groups. It appeared they were fleeing. They were heading for the river, after leaving the area where the Koancho agent was disposed of.

Sakei was intrigued by this development. They had to have something of value. Otherwise, a small army wouldn't be hunting down two people. Not with grenades and automatic weapons.

He'd be interested in finding out just who they were. If the reports about the mixed bag of intruders from the cliff-top clearing accurate, there had to have been some sort of exchange going on between two formerly hostile forces. Sakei didn't need many leaps of logic to realize that one or both of the pair might be hostages held by one side in trade for something delivered by the other.

Which only sweetened the pot for Sakei to put an end to

the invaders running around his woods. He could use whatever two groups were bartering toward his own ends. Most likely, it would be cash to contribute toward his war funds.

The freshly deposited corpses that had been left so nicely for them by the Yakuza over time were coming to the end of their test incubation cycle. If he was right in his efforts, the pathogens he'd developed would act as a disease vector even when left dormant in dead flesh. Sailing dead bodies into the water reservoirs of major cities would unleash a plague of epic proportions.

It was the only reason he'd allowed the Yazuka to trespass, unhindered, in the first place. Now, it seemed that Sakei would be able to use an even fresher batch of corpses to dispense his death spores.

He wondered who they would turn out to be.

HOGAN AND MACHIDA LED the group through the woods at a frenetic pace. Nobody was cutting them off from the front, but that didn't mean that they weren't keeping an eye open for trouble to attack from both sides.

The valley hid more treachery than the simple betrayal and backbiting that Hogan had prepared for. A defending army had popped up out of nowhere and killed two of his mercenaries and three of Machida's thugs.

Hogan could feel that more lives would be lost today. He'd heard from the team he sent after the Anthony girl and Cooper that another three men were down from the combined force. The forest was quickly becoming a deathtrap, and he wondered how much longer he could afford to stick around and look for her.

He looked at Machida. The emotions in his face were hard to read. But he was sure the Yakuza man was sharing the exact same confusion he was. They were temporary allies, but once they had gotten over their latest challenges, they would be enemies again.

He didn't believe for a moment that Machida was interested in sharing the potential for Anthony's weapons designs with anyone else. Splitting ownership would only mean that neither side could truly afford to write its own payday for the final results. Competitive sales on the black market would only serve to make them lose money as they tried to underbid each other.

Frustration dug at his gut, stirring the hot embers of a burning rage that he wanted to unleash. Lashing out in fury was a release he longed to have. Emptying a full magazine into Cooper, even if only into the FBI agent's dead body, would give Hogan the kind of satisfaction he needed.

"This man, Cooper. When you spoke of his abilities, you spoke with respect," Machida said as they walked toward a gap in the woods.

"He was good enough to fight off six men in the confines of a van," Hogan replied. "And he eluded my men long enough to reach the rendezvous and cause this fucking headache."

"So that implies skill and determination," Machida replied. He paused at the tree line and pulled out his phone.

"Who're you calling?" Hogan asked.

"My men have called me," the Yakuza man told him.

He broke into a rapid flurry of Japanese, far faster than Hogan could follow with his limited skill. Machida put the phone away with a scowl. Over his own tactical network, he received a quick message, and he figured it was similar to the one Machida had received. The party that went after Cooper and the girl had just picked up a tail in the woods.

The marauders were stalking them.

"At least they're not that stealthy," Hogan grumbled.

"Don't engage them unless you have a good, clear line of fire. Then take them out, fast and dirty."

"That was my suggestion as well," Machida said.

Hogan narrowed his eyes. "Good thinking, there. We know that we're being tailed, but we haven't seen anyone on our back trail. So that means they're not that close. Either way, let's not lose our lead."

Machida's face had frozen into a grim, solid mask.

"What's wrong?" Hogan asked.

"This is the area where we buried the men we killed," Machida responded.

"Which men?" Hogan asked, looking at the clearing, seeing several freshly dug-up, shallow graves. "Holy shit."

"This is where we dump a good portion of our enemies," Machida answered. "Only the most recent have been brought up."

"What the hell?" Hogan asked. "What kind of sickos would do that?"

"Someone who needed fresh human cadavers. Perhaps for experimentation," Machida mused.

There was a click over Hogan's earpiece and he dropped lower into a crouch. "The enemy's approaching from the rear. Closing in on us."

Machida's lips formed a tight, hard line. "Should we stay and fight or move on?"

"My men have armor. We'll settle into the graves. You take your men to the other side of the clearing and set up there to give us cover fire from the tree line," Hogan said. "We'll take out these guys and have at least one set of thorns out of our ass."

Machida nodded, and he waved his Yakuza troops to his side. Hogan knew that his mercenaries had heard his plan over the headsets they wore. They were already in transit to the clearing, laying themselves in the shallow graves, taking cover behind mounds of dirt and leaves to disguise their presence.

Machida's Yakuza force was equally quick and efficient, taking cover behind tree trunks, crouching low enough to be obfuscated by the tall grasses, but ready to lend their considerable firepower to Hogan's team.

Hogan thought for a moment about how easy it would be for Machida to break and run, or to shoot him in the back, but then he would be stuck with facing the mysterious defenders of this valley all alone. Hogan knew that the third force was indeed a lucky break, an extra bit of security in a deadly balance of power.

But soon enough, they were going to have to deal with each other.

That settled uneasily in Hogan's gut, like an angry viper, coiled to strike.

BOLAN STOPPED HONEY and pushed her behind cover as they were within sight of the river. The girl looked at him, her blue eyes wide with terrified alertness.

"Good grief, what's got you spooked now?" she asked softly, low enough so her words wouldn't carry past the rustle of the bushes and tree branches in the breeze. Her gaze extended toward the river.

"It's too open. We'll keep to the trees unless absolutely necessary," Bolan told her. "I'd prefer to have the coverage of tree trunks when the lead flies."

"You don't strike me as the kind of man who hides from danger."

"I don't. But I also know I'm not bulletproof," Bolan told her. He took a few deep breaths. The pain from his injuries was fading, but he wasn't certain if it was from numbness, exhaustion or nerve damage.

"You're sweating and pale," Honey noted.

Bolan wiped his brow and knew that he was overheating. The blood loss from his shoulder and perspiration from exertion were combining to dehydrate him. Unfortunately, the web belt he'd gotten off the dead man contained no water bottles. He looked at the still creek ahead of him and contemplated the safety of drinking from the stagnant water. If it were a running body of water, he knew that the water would be far more likely to be fresh. Here, there was a possibility that algae and other organisms had accumulated to make him even worse off if he attempted to drink.

"We're not drinking that water," Bolan told her. He glanced upstream and saw something that gave him an idea. He pulled his knife and grabbed a handful of grass, slicing it free. He popped the plants into his mouth and began to chew. It was bitter, but the juices from the blades gushed in his mouth with each grind of his teeth. He spit out the wad once he'd felt it grow tough and stringy.

"You don't think that river's healthy?"

"Silt and algae look thick in it from here. Who's to tell what kind of organisms are in it."

"And grass is okay?" Honey asked.

Bolan pointed the tip of his knife up the river a way. A pair of deer were nibbling the grass, but staying away from the water's edge. "If they can eat it, it's not poisonous."

Bolan handed her a tuft of grass. "Just chew it, then spit it out."

"Why?" she asked.

"Your throat's not tough enough for grass. And then, even if you did manage to swallow it without scratching up your esophagus, the grass would punch through your digestive system like a freight train. We don't have time to be held up by stomach cramps," Bolan explained.

Honey chewed, looking at him askance. She had to agree with his assessment. The cellulose in the grass was rough and harsh, not like lettuce or celery.

Bolan was on his third mouthful when he suddenly stopped chewing and spat. Honey was confused for a moment, but then looked to see the deer taking off, darting away across the river, their hooves splashing in the shallow water.

"We've got company coming," Bolan said. "This way."

She fell into step behind him, and he led her into the woods. They were out of sight from the river when she heard splashes in the water and gunshots ringing out.

A voice called out in Japanese. Honey frowned at the sound.

"What did he say?" Bolan whispered.

"He said for them to stop shooting at the deer," she answered softly.

"We owe those deer," Bolan replied. "They gave us refreshment, and they distracted our enemy."

"Remind me to send them a nice postcard," Honey answered. "Do you even have a plan, Cooper? I'm not that good at traipsing around the woods, and I'm sure I'm a terrible shot."

"Don't worry. I'll lead you to a safe place, and then I'll do what I have to do."

"And what's that?"

"My priority became the cult the minute we learned about them from Chiba," he explained. "Sure, we have the Yakuza and Hogan to worry about, but they're not as big a threat as the Black Serpent."

Honey nodded. "But you're all alone."

"I'll figure something out," Bolan reassured her. "This is nothing new for me."

Honey looked back toward the river. "So that's why you have all those cool scars."

Bolan took her hand, holding the Uzi in the other. "Come on."

MACHIDA WILLED HIMSELF to deadly calm. The tremors in his hands faded and his heart stilled, its beat no longer wild and rampant. The twin Berettas he held were unwavering extensions of his will once more. The fear and anticipation of the coming ambush and battle were not going to intimidate him into uselessness.

He glanced among the tree trunks. His men were secured in their positions, weapons at the ready. When their frightened eyes looked toward him, they would find a calm and resolute leader. Suddenly, the tough, ultra-hip and deadly Japanese street soldiers were no longer in command.

Sure enough, an uncertain face met his. Machida, his features a mask of determination, nodded back. The message flashed between them as if it were written in lightning across the heavens.

*You will not fail. I command you.*

Machida braced one of his wrists against the notch where the trunk split into two slender stalks before rising up twenty feet over his head. He had an excellent improvised turret with which to survey the clearing. He spotted Hogan and his men reaching on their harnesses for black spheres.

They would throw grenades against the tree line the minute they had a target.

A devastating opening gambit, Machida mused. He waved to the others, alerting them that Hogan's men were up to something. He returned to focusing through the break of the bifurcated trunk, watching for the advance of their enemy.

The next moments dragged, slowly, painfully. His heart started to pound again.

When he spotted the first shadow, he had to hold back from pulling the trigger on his Beretta. To shoot too soon would be to ruin the ambush against the mystery soldiers.

Hogan threw the first grenade, others sailing heartbeats later, the little round spheres launching into the trees in a formation, like a flock of geese.

However, geese didn't detonate with tooth-rattling force. The blasts tore through the tree line and screams filled the air. Automatic gunfire blazed away almost instantly, and a bullet crashed into the trunk Machida hid behind. He waited until he spotted a running shadow through the trees and pulled the trigger on his Beretta, pumping out 9 mm rounds. Hogan's men opened up too, and autofire ripped at Machida's target, killing him dozens of times over. Machida looked for fresh targets, his Yakuza gunners firing at anything they could see.

The clearing was one constant thunderstorm of exploding grenades and blasting bullets. Dying screams filled the air for a moment, but cut off soon after. Machida winced as a bullet glanced off the trunk of his tree. He felt blood on his ear and knew that the bullet had nicked him. It burned slightly, but he didn't stop shooting. His gun ran empty, and he switched Berettas, continuing to blast away with the full pistol.

One of the Yakuza gunners jerked, part of his face disappearing in a cloud of crimson-tinted darkness. At first Machida thought the man had caught a bullet fired from the other side of the clearing. He looked at the wounded man more carefully. Sticking to his face was a spiked ball, the tines jammed through his cheek and eye. The Yakuza gunman pawed weakly at his face as gouts of blood poured down from his punctured features. Somewhere, in the back of his mind, the name of the spiked ball came to mind. It was a *joarare*, a "hailstone."

Machida didn't have to wait long to figure out where the

weapon came from. He spun in time to see a *yari* spear spike into the back of another of his men. A figure in black BDUs and Kevlar held the deadly *yari* as the point tore into the heart of his man. Machida whirled and hammered off three shots from his Beretta, two bullets plunking harmlessly into the chest of the man, the third slug shearing into his jaw, splitting it in an explosion of blood and gore.

The Yakuza headman didn't have time to celebrate his victory. Another attacker charged toward him, swinging a length of chain, a heavy iron weight at one end. The *kusari* tore open the bark of the tree where Machida had stood only a moment before. The heavy weighted end gouged away splinters and wood two inches deep in the trunk. Machida ducked as the twelve-foot-long chain swirled again, lashing at him. Machida swung his Beretta into play, firing out the rest of his clip at the attacker. His rounds found only Kevlar body armor in the panicked burst of fire.

The *kusari*-wielding attacker was still stunned by the flurry of bullets rattling against his chest, and his third whiplash strike punched the weighted end of the chain into the ground inches from Machida's foot. The Yakuza man dropped his Beretta and grabbed the swinging weapon. He yanked hard, twisting the length of the chain around him as leverage to pop it free.

His enemy held on tight, pulling back with all of his strength. Machida growled and spun back to face him. All around the Yakuza team leader, attackers were battling it out with his men. They had been taken off guard.

Machida realized the assailants were carrying machine pistols strapped over their shoulders. The assassins were trying to take out as many of their prey from surprise, using silent, but no less deadly weapons, before having to resort to louder guns that would give them away.

The *kusari*-wielding attacker stopped struggling for his chain weapon, instead choosing to grope for the pistol in his thigh holster. Machida snapped the chain quickly, and a wave of steel ripped up its length and crashed hard against the intruder's head and face. Flesh tore, laying bare cheek and jawbones and gleeming red-tinted white from the horrific damage of steel against skin. The chainman's hands rose to his gory, bloodied features. Machida swung the *kusari* again, wrapping the chain around his enemy's neck. With a hard yank, he felt the vibrations of crunching bone along the length of the steel.

The attacker slumped to the ground. Machida lunged for the downed corpse, clawing at the submachine gun strapped to the dead body.

"Hogan!" Machida bellowed, finally getting his thoughts back together. Bullets tore through the air, the thunder of automatic fire ripping into Machida's consciousness.

A blast of gunfire issued from the clearing, missing Machida by only a foot, but tearing into another attacker lunging from the trees. The man jerked and danced as bullets punched into his body armor, then he finally flew backward as the end of the extended burst chopped into his face. Machida got the Uzi free from the corpse and tore away a pair of spare magazines, tucking them into his pocket.

Hogan was crouched against the tree Machida had used as a turret only minutes before. He held his assault weapon in both hands, one side of his face streaked with blood.

"Let's get out of here!" Hogan bellowed. He swung his submachine gun and triggered it, slashing an arc of fire across the legs of another of their mysterious enemies, throwing him facedown to the ground. The pistol and katana in the wounded man's hands flew from his grasp as he struck the forest floor.

Machida scanned the clearing. Half of the men that Hogan

had laid in ambush with were still in their holes, now lifeless, killed in graves meant for other men, their bodies slumped forever in mute testimony to the savagery and completeness of the enemy assault. Machida swept his Uzi in an arc, looking for survivors among his own men, and found three embattled, battered men. Hogan had four with him.

The battle seemed over; no one else was standing.

"Tell your men to grab something heavier than those bolt actions," Hogan told him. "We need firepower. These guys are too much."

"This is all that survived?" Machida asked. He slung the Uzi long enough to bend and pick up the fallen pistol and katana. He rummaged through the injured man's belt and took his spare magazines. Suddenly the wounded attacker reached up, clutching Machida's pants leg.

Pain- and fear-filled eyes burned up at him. Machida cocked the sword, raising it to bring it down on the man. He paused. It wasn't an attack. The man was clinging to him, looking for mercy.

The rattle of submachine gun fire split the air, and in the same instant, the man's face disintegrated into a pulpy mass of destroyed bone, brain and tissue.

"If you're going to hang on to that sword, Machida, you best fucking use it. I hate wasting ammunition," Hogan growled.

Machida glared at the mercenary. If he weren't already fighting for his life against two enemies, he'd have killed him. But he needed Hogan's remaining men as a buffer to bolster his forces.

At least until he found the Anthony girl.

Then he'd get out of this murderous forest.

What he did after that, he'd leave up to the dictates of his personal honor.

## 6

Bolan almost missed the seismic ground sensor as he lead Honey through the woods. However, the wire-thin antenna glinted dully in a shaft of light that cut through the treetop cover. It was mere chance that they passed by the sensor at the time of day when the sun was at the right angle, and they were in the right position to pick up the reflection along the length of the metal.

The Executioner stopped and approached the device.

"What the hell is that?" Honey asked.

"The forest is wired," Bolan explained. "That's a seismic sensor."

Honey looked at the unit that Bolan uncovered. "You sure that's not from some kind of Japanese earthquake watch?"

"This is too far from the population, and why would it be so hidden? Besides, the device isn't Japanese made," Bolan explained. He pointed to the English writing on the side. "This is from an American security company."

"Security?"

"It will pick up footsteps. You wouldn't need more than fifty of these sensors to mine and observe activity in the whole valley."

Honey stepped back. "Oh this is just great! Those guys who killed that government agent, the guy who grabbed me, they've been tracking us?"

Bolan nodded grimly. "Us, Hogan's men, the Yakuza. They know where we all are. They're probably using the information to flank us."

Honey looked around.

"Not yet," Bolan said.

Honey thought back to the distant sound of gunfire only moments ago. "They'll be able to hunt down everyone in this valley."

Bolan felt around the sensor. It had no additions or modifications, especially booby traps, attached. He ripped the antenna out of the sensor, throwing it away into the weeds. "Now we know about their advantage."

"But they can still see us, and we can't see them," Honey said.

Bolan shook his head. "Their advantage was that we didn't know we were being watched and followed. Now, we know that they can hear us by our footsteps."

"So we tread lightly?" Honey asked.

Bolan closed his eyes. He knew that taking out one sensor would only produce a small blind zone, one far smaller than the area the sensor was supposed to cover. Other sensors would overlap, leaving only a precision area for repairmen and a security team to close in on as soon as the seismic device stopped transmitting back to headquarters. He doubted the hole he made was more than a twenty-foot diameter in the overall coverage of the valley.

Bolan was counting on the forces of Hogan and Machida running around the valley. With them, the Black Serpents wouldn't have enough manpower to afford an on the spot repair of a single blackout. He regretted not finding any radios on the trio of men who had tortured Chiba to death. His Japanese wasn't fluent in the least, but Honey would probably be able to decipher. He doubted that she had lived in

Japan off and on for four years without learning enough of the language to get by.

He caught movement out of the corner of his eye. Turning, he brought up his Uzi. "Time to move," he whispered.

"You think it's the death cult?" Honey asked as they cut through the woods.

"It would be too soon for them to respond to something as minor as the loss of a sensor, especially with our other friends on the hunt in these woods," Bolan told her. "Our trackers may have doubled back and found our trail. Or it's possible that we might have attracted the attention of a hunting squad."

"We were right on top of the sensor for long enough to attract attention," Honey suggested.

"Either way, let's not stick around long enough to find out who's trying to kill us."

The Executioner pointed Honey toward a path and crouched at a tree trunk, scanning their back trail. The shadow of a human figure passed between the trees about twenty yards away. Not near enough for the sounds of Bolan and Honey's low voices to have carried to alert them, but close enough for them to spot either of the two black-clad figures if they were alert enough.

Honey hissed. Bolan glanced toward her. He saw two figures up the path and pushed her down behind a bush.

Bolan had expected the Black Serpents to be more preoccupied with the presence of the larger intruding forces, but obviously they had sent out a team specifically for the two of them. There was no time to worry about underestimating the size and thoroughness of the death cult, though. He had to somehow take care of his pursuers fast enough to keep Honey from coming to harm.

If he was lucky, he would be in for a windfall of acquired equipment as well.

But first, he needed to lay an ambush.

He couldn't count on Honey as being a good distraction. Perhaps with Hogan or Machida, as they would still view her as valuable property, but even then, Bolan would be loathe to use a human being as bait. More often, it was the Executioner's battle strategy to lay himself out for the enemy to come after him. At least then he had control as to whether the bait lived or died, and if he lost in the conflict, he hadn't risked the life of a soldier on the same side or an innocent bystander.

"Give me the shotgun, Honey," Bolan whispered. "And then hide in the rut under those roots."

Honey blanched at the thought of being unarmed. Bolan handed over his Walther, flicking off the safety.

"You can use this to protect yourself if things go bad, but I'm going to make sure the fight doesn't come your way," Bolan told her. "I just need to make some noise to attract their attention."

Honey took the pistol and put her thumb on the hammer.

"No, don't cock it. It'll fire with a stiff pull of the trigger," he informed her.

Honey looked down at the gun and wrapped her hand tight around the grip.

"Right. Now sit tight," Bolan whispered.

Bolan slung the Uzi, and, gripping the shotgun with both hands, crawled into the forest path. The men who were trying to flank them from the front were visible now, but they were looking straight ahead, and not at the slithering form of the Executioner on the forest floor. He propped up his shotgun.

There was no front sight on the sawed-off cannon, but Bolan was able to index along the top of the barrel, bisecting the body of his first target with the black, cavernous tube of the barrel. A pull of the trigger jolted the weapon hard in the Executioner's hands, the roar of the weapon tearing through the still, uncertain silence of the woods.

The swarm of buckshot slashed violently across the space between Bolan and his prey. Multiple shot balls tore into the arm and side of the man, and he whirled. The arm itself was hanging, a ragged ruin as pellets had sliced through biceps and imbedded in bone. The man screamed, dropping his gun, but he was still standing, his body armor protecting his torso from violation by the volley of pellets launched by the roaring shotgun.

Bolan tromboned the slide of the shotgun and aimed higher. His second shattering blast smashed the face completely off the wounded gunman's skull. The second gunman spun, looking for the source of the sudden ambush. He held down the trigger on his Ingram submachine gun, sweeping the trees at chest height.

Bolan aimed lower, directing his fire at the pelvis of the second shooter. Again the shotgun boomed, and the deadly salvo of buckshot pellets smashed the man's hip and pelvis. Blood spurted as the femoral artery was severed by the force of breaking bone and hurtling missiles slicing through yielding flesh. The gunman screamed, thrashing on the ground, all thoughts of further combat completely forgotten as he bled to death.

The racket brought the others running, and the Executioner rolled behind the cover of a tree trunk. The position shift was just in time, as divots of earth were chewed out of the ground by the Black Serpents' automatic weapons. Bolan fisted the Uzi, rising to a crouch. He poked the barrel around the tree and targeted the lead gunner, aiming for his face and upper torso before tapping off a short burst. He wanted to conserve his ammunition, and his marksmanship served him well as 9 mm bullets struck the cultist through the nose and right eye.

The man tumbled to the ground, but his partner whipped his submachine gun around and triggered a long burst. Automatic fire chewed the tree trunk that Bolan had been hiding behind only moments before. However, the big American was now flat on his chest, the Uzi extended, both hands on the gun. He triggered a burst into the gunman, aiming too low, too quickly. The 115-grain hardball rounds plunked into the Black Serpent's body armor, serving only to give the shooter pause.

In the moment between Bolan's evaluation of his first shot and pulling the trigger on his second burst, the stunned gunman suddenly jerked from the side. The Japanese killer's shoulder exploded in a spray of red, and his hair flew up. Bolan's next three rounds tore into the injured man's throat and jaw, obliterating the lower part of his face.

The Executioner rose to a crouch and looked at the man he blasted in the pelvis with the shotgun. The wounded fighter had rolled onto his good hip and struggled to bring his weapon to bear. Bolan leveled his Uzi at the dying man and swept his head and shoulders with a withering burst of 9 mm slugs.

"Honey?" Bolan called out softly. He jogged toward where he'd left her, and saw her, the Walther trembling uneasily in her hand. Her blue eyes were wide with fear.

"I'm sorry. I was afraid that you wouldn't stop him before he shot you," Honey said. The slide on the Walther was locked back, the gun empty. Out of nine shots, she'd connected with two. It wasn't a bad effort, but it was something that shook the young woman to her core.

He took the Walther gently from her and placed a reassuring hand on her shoulder.

"It's okay, Honey."

Honey's face went from shocked to furious. "You know, it used to be cool to think that people would be killing each other for me."

"What?" Bolan asked.

"You know, having suitors fucking each other up for me. Life and death, all at my whim, with me as the cause," Honey growled. Her teeth were grit, and her knuckles were white where she clenched her fists.

"It's not so much fun now that it's really happening, is it?" Bolan asked.

Honey's blue eyes were unblinking. Bolan could tell that having her fantasies stripped away was pulling down the calloused cynicism that guarded her world. "No. It's not any fun. I hate this shit."

"It's not all clean like in the movies," Bolan told her.

Honey snorted. "You haven't been watching the same movies I have."

"I don't doubt that. Listen, if I had my way, no one would have to kill anyone else," Bolan told her.

Her eyes searched his, but she found no lie.

The anger in the girl's features melted away.

"Okay. I think I'm cool now," she said softly, looking down. Her teeth clinked against her lower lip's two piercings, as her brow furrowed in concentration. Bolan gave her shoulder another squeeze, letting her know she wasn't alone.

"We have to move," Bolan said. "I'm going to need your help first."

"With what?" Honey asked.

"I want to get you in some body armor," he explained. "And I want to use their radio and GPS tracking gear. We also need spare ammunition."

Honey looked at the dead bodies. "Great. More dead bodies."

"Just hold on to whatever I give to you," Bolan said.

"Okay," Honey answered.

"Good, I want to put some layers of Kevlar between you and death."

Honey nodded. She stared at the corpses on the ground, her face hardening the more the looked at them. It was just like the gory pictures she looked at on the Internet, the dead bodies shown on TV screens at the Goth clubs she went to. She could watch marathons of movies where people were butchered and mutilated, she should have been more prepared. But this was real. This was in her face. But she kept on steeling herself against it. "You're used to this shit, bitch. Quit being such a goddamn fairy princess and get hard."

Bolan gave her shoulder a squeeze. "That's it. Hang tough."

It wasn't as if the girl had much of a choice. She waited while Bolan got everything he needed.

"LORD ZAKOJI!" Rikyu cried out.

Sakei turned, reacting to the sound of his title, the name he assumed when he took up the leadership of the Burakku Uwibami clan. The organization had survived in one form or another for the past five hundred years, devoted to the twin causes of isolating Japan and ruling the island nation under an iron fist. At first, the cultists had been more interested in fighting off the influences of China and other Asian nations in their isolationist policies. Back then, it was an easier struggle to remain alive and strong, even against the shogunate, and there were always young, disenfranchised men willing to shed blood in the name of striking back at a vaguely defined enemy.

That was the true power of the Burakku Uwibami, and Sakei knew it was the same kind of power that motivated the blind mewling masses populating every group from the American Ku Klux Klan to Palestinian freedom fighters on the West Bank.

Deny people certain rights, or make them feel invaded and turned into second-class citizens, and you'll have ripe grounds to recruit from. Fear of foreigners, illegalization of a certain drink or drug, denial of economic status. It all fed into the massive engine that laid seige to humanity, providing the greedy and skilled few with the manpower to increase their wealth, their power, their prestige.

"Lord Zakoji! We've lost contact with the hunting team that went after the two who broke away from the clearing," Rikyu reported.

Sakei grimaced, shaking his head. "Our other teams?"

"Umon reported that they tried to flank the enemy," Rikyu stated. "But nine of them escaped."

"And the other intruders?" Sakei asked. "The second group?"

"We're still tracking them. We're hoping they will lead us to the two escapees."

Sakei ruminated on that. "Why? We should be able to track them ourselves."

"They've disappeared for the time being," Rikyu stated.

"Disappeared?"

Rikyu looked uncomfortable. "One of the seismic sensors has gone dead. Right in the place where we lost contact with Hanma's team."

"Hanma was the one you sent after the two runners?"

Rikyu nodded.

"Damnation."

Sakei moved to the window of his office. "I want all guard shifts at the ready. No breaks. If anyone tries to penetrate the compound, I want them to step into a meat grinder."

Rikyu nodded. *"Hai."* He left to convey Sakei's orders.

Sakei realized the situation was rapidly growing out of his control.

His men were adequately trained with firearms as well as martial-arts weapons. It was the only way to compromise their need to be an effective fighting force and their desire to return Japan to its old ways.

Sakei was realistic. He knew that in a straight-up fight, his men wouldn't be a match for heavily armed mercenaries, special forces soldiers or counterterrorism-trained police operatives. They were taught well enough to protect themselves, and he had enough men to make any assault on his compound a costly one. Hidden explosives around the base, set off on command, would also increase the destruction against enemies who attacked, but if the enemy outnumbered his men, then they would fall like wheat before a scythe.

It wasn't going to be easy, and yet, Sakei was expecting this enemy force to be on its last legs. If they were going to receive backup, the whole battle could go against him.

Then there was the wild card.

The mysterious twosome that eliminated a four-man team and discovered one of his seismic sensors.

Every instinct in Sakei told him that this pair was going to be the deciding force.

Even deeper, he sensed that there was a great difference about at least one of them. He could feel the presence, an ancient driving force that rumbled through the valley like thunder. This was no ordinary man.

Could it be the true shogun's executioner, reborn and coming to face his destiny against the heir of Lord Zakoji after four centuries?

The thought at once chilled and brought a calm to Sakei. He had taken on the mantle of the ancient alchemist warrior who fought against the shogunate in order to recruit an army to bring about the downfall of the modern, soulless government of Japan.

The time was rapidly approaching. Zakoji was going to make war with the westernized Japan, but now an obstacle was rising to face him. It was a battle that was foretold nearly half a millennia ago. Whether the prophecy would be truth, or the empty, hollow curse of a failed, dying man, that was what Sakei doubted.

And knowing that doubt, Sakei rebuked himself. He knew that it would take far more than guns and swords to defeat this executioner.

It would take faith, confidence and a fire of the heart.

A fire that was chilled by fear of the mystery man.

**7**

Desmond Nickles was distracted from his original mission. He'd been out by Hogan with a mixed force of mercenaries and Japanese mobsters to hunt for Rebecca Anthony and Special Agent Matt Cooper the minute they made their escape, while Hogan stayed with the Yakuza boss to figure out who the psycho with the Uzi was. The whole mess had spiraled out of control, and as he gripped his M-16/M-203 tightly, he remembered with chilling clarity the ambush Cooper had pulled off, killing three of his number.

Even a 40 mm grenade hadn't proved enough to wipe that turkey off the face of the planet. Nickles tried to explain it away by careful use of cover and being a couple degrees off in his aim with the launcher. The excuses didn't quite cover the fact that one man had managed to not only pin down a dozen men, but to kill four of them.

Unno, the leader of the Yakuza contingent that Machida sent with him, gripped his long-barreled revolver tightly, eyes scanning hard to pierce the thick woodlands around them, searching for signs of their prey.

"Nickles," he heard Hogan over his earpiece.

"Here. What's wrong?" Nickles asked.

"We took a hammering. I've only got four of our team left," Hogan answered. "Where are you?"

Nickles flipped his wrist and checked the map case strapped to his arm. He read off his coordinates.

"We'll try to hook up," Hogan said.

Unno was talking on his cell phone, presumably with Machida.

"Right, Top. Got any other messages for me?" he asked.

Nickles thought it might be time for him to use the satellite phone to call in their backup. He would be able to do that surreptitiously with just a simple press of the speed dial. A pre-programmed code would bring in help by helicopter.

"Yeah. Call Mother and tell her we'll be late for dinner," Hogan answered.

Nickles confirmed Hogan's order. Once help came, they'd be able to outnumber and overpower the Yakuza strike force. The minute they were out of the way, and the psychos holed up in this valley were wiped out, Hogan and the mercenary team would grab Rebecca Anthony and get the hell out.

Nickles was sick of looking at trees and jumping at shadows. He wanted to be in a bar, licking wine off the tits of a topless hoochie girl.

Unno suddenly crouched and froze. Nickles reacted instantly, lowering his profile as well. All along the line, men dropped to stooped postures to make themselves smaller targets.

"Down there," Unno said in English.

Nickles narrowed his eyes and spotted a row of fallen tree trunks.

"Saw movement," Unno added, his voice softer.

"It better not be more fucking deer," Nickles grumbled. He thumbed a fresh 40 mm grenade into his launcher.

The Yakuza man smiled at the American.

Nickles smiled back, then tried to quash the feeling. Finding the man likable might give him pause when it came time to pull the trigger on Unno. Unno had returned his attention to the row of fallen trees. Nickles took the opportunity to reach back to the satellite phone and thumb on the power button. It was muted, so it didn't beep on activation—the Yazuka wouldn't be alerted to the change in plans. Another press of his thumb, and he hit the keys to transmit to the helicopter crew. In another heartbeat, he flicked off the phone and brought his free hand back to the grenade launcher. All the while he watched Unno, making sure his eyes were still on their mutual prize.

"Unno, take your men farther along the ridge. Keep to cover but make some noise. Attract his attention. We'll slip around the other side," Nickles ordered.

Nickles led his surviving mercenaries down the hilltop line, rounding a bend in the gully. He wasn't going to risk his men without the benefit of a distraction, superior numbers and firepower or not.

The memory of Cooper's fighting prowess was burned into his memory as if etched there with acid.

Nickles sighted through the scope atop his weapon and spotted the shadow of one figure. His finger took up the slack on the M-16's trigger, but he stopped when he saw the distinctive purple streaks in Honey Anthony's blond hair. He held his fire.

Where the hell was Cooper?

He swept the scope across the gully, looking in the shadows of the logs. There was no sign of him, but from his angle, he didn't have a view of one end of the trunks. Honey slipped towards the end of one of the fallen trees, tucking herself out of his sight.

Nickles's jaw set angrily.

The wily special agent had disappeared on them.

"Anybody see Cooper?" he asked.

His team had spread out. They were far enough apart not to be hit by a single burst of automatic fire, but still within hearing distance of a whisper. The other mercenaries indicated that they hadn't seen their armed quarry, communicating with shakes of their heads.

"All right. Slow and easy. First sign of trouble, light it up," Nickles stated.

The trained gunmen paused, and Nickles knew that he couldn't blame them one bit. Fear gripped them each in a tenacious tangle of anticipation.

How could one man hold them in such terror?

Nickles dropped his hand to the trigger of the grenade launcher. Damn getting the girl back. He wasn't going to risk his life against the deadly Agent Cooper.

He tightened his finger on the grenade launcher's trigger when he caught a flicker of movement. A dark, flat shape rose from the shadow of one tree trunk, a flash flickering from its center. Too late, Desmond Nickles realized what it was as 9 mm slugs danced up his chest and tore into his throat. One final flash of crimson, and the mercenary saw no more.

THE EXECUTIONER SWUNG his Uzi's muzzle from the man with the grenade launcher even as the gunner's corpse tumbled lifelessly to the ground. The leaves Honey had dumped over his prone figure fell away, fluttering in the breeze as he rose. To the surviving mercenaries, it was as if he rocketed out of the ground, bursting from the very earth itself like some forest demon come to life. Damp leaves still stuck to his face and hair.

Panic fire sizzled past Bolan, bullets hammering into rotted wood and detonating spongy chunks and soggy splinters as they struck. Bolan counted on the element of his surprise appearance to buy him a few seconds, swiveling the submachine gun's muzzle to empty another burst into the face of a second mercenary. The 9 mm slugs eradicated the man's features in a blossoming flower of gore and bone.

Two down, three to go. That still left the Yakuza gunmen who were behind him. He knew a couple enemies eliminated didn't guaruntee the rest of the course of battle, and he had to work fast to finish this side of the skirmish before the Japanese mobsers swept down.

Bolan dived to the side as the trio of surviving armored mercenaries opened up. He felt one 9 mm slug pluck at his abdomen, but it was a glancing blow off the Kevlar body armor that was too small for the Executioner's torso. The Velcro snaps barely managed to wrap around his rib cage, and each breath strained the seal between the hook and pile of the straps.

Bolan hit the ground and felt a seam pop, tearing free under his shoulder. Enemy fire lanced the air, missing him completely. Bolan let the strap flop, focusing his attention on a third target. His first burst was low, peppering the Kevlar of his opponent. Before Bolan could adjust his aim, the enemy gunman swung behind a tree trunk, seeking cover.

One of the other mercenaries lobbed a black sphere, his throw leaving him a sitting duck for the Executioner's next burst of gunfire. The 9 mm salvo from the Uzi missed the man's head, but chopped into his unprotected arm. Muscle and bone tore under Bolan's fire and the grenade-throwing gunman spun away, howling from the pain of his wounds.

Bolan spun and charged, running along the top of one of the logs. His long legs pushed him away from the dropping grenade, but he knew that he wasn't going to get far enough from the minibomb. He lunged, taking to the air and diving toward the gap between two fallen trunks. A rifle round zipped from the third remaining mercenary, skipping along

Bolan's raw, wounded shoulder. Fresh pain poured into his back as he struck the ground. The Kevlar prevented a crippling injury, but the force knocked the wind out of Bolan, pinning his stunned body to the ground.

The grenade detonated, shaking the air with a thunderous roar that battered Bolan's ears. Debris struck his head and back in a steady rain of wood chunks, dirt and leaves, once more covering him with clutter. It wouldn't help now to camouflage him—the enemy already knew where he was—and Bolan fought with his unresponsive arms to get up and moving.

Shots rang out from where Honey Anthony had taken cover. Bolan suspected that the Yakuza gunmen were coming down, attracted by the sounds of battle. Bolan looked up and saw two targets out in the open, crabwalking down the hill in halting steps to keep from slipping on the slope.

Finally Bolan's hands responded to his will, bringing up the Uzi. His limbs still felt numb, and he doubted he had anything resembling fine motor control, but his finger squashed down on the trigger. A line of impacts erupted to the left of the two Yakuza gunmen, but to the Executioner's satisfaction, some of the slugs slashed across the legs of one of the Japanese mobsters. The man screamed and toppled in a crash of twisting limbs.

Then the Uzi ran dry.

Bolan squeezed the magazine catch on the grip of the machine pistol with a numbed thumb, sliding the empty clip free of the pistol grip's well. He glanced back, knowing that the two uninjured mercenaries weren't going to let this opportunity pass. Even though they didn't know he was operating with dead, wooden limbs, an empty weapon was an advantage they could press. Bullets ripped the logs on either side of him.

His hand tore at the magazine pouch, squeezing the connector clip that held the pocket closed. Ordinarily, with full manual dexterity, he would have been able to pop the release and yank a magazine free in the space of a couple seconds, but his insensate fingers felt as if they were working with mush. Finally, the release clicked after two eternity-long seconds of incoming fire.

Where was Honey? The Yakuza gunmen on the hill had retreated under the Executioner's first answering fire to their advance, but they wouldn't be kept at bay for long.

The girl was wearing body armor too, as they had found a vest that fit her. Bolan didn't delude himself, though. Honey might have been afforded some protection against gunfire, but a Kevlar vest wouldn't make her invincible.

The clip came free, and Bolan brought it up to the magazine well of the Uzi. He bumped his hand with the first stab into the slot, then after a second thrust, the magazine was in place. He grabbed the cocking knob atop the Uzi and racked it back. His fingers were growing steadily more responsive to his wishes, and Bolan scanned the hillside.

"Honey?" he called out.

"Still alive," she called back.

The hillside was still empty of Yakuza gunmen, and Bolan took the opportunity to roll onto his back and focus on the mercenaries.

The gunman with the wounded arm lurched into view, holding his machine pistol with one hand. The weapon sparked and barked, spitting its payload toward the downed warrior. Bolan triggered his Uzi, catching the gunman across his thighs. The man dropped onto his face, his weapon popping free from his grip.

Bolan fired a second burst, catching the fallen gunman in the back of his skull, shearing away the bone and finishing him off. It was a life-and-death battle. Every living enemy meant that Honey could be captured or harmed.

An innocent girl's life was at stake, and the mercenaries had cast their lot by their actions. They were trained killers who were willing to resort to kidnapping and blackmail, taking Honey's well-being into their hands like some sort of toy.

One of the mercenaries, the one armed with a 9 mm submachine gun, charged the corpse of Bolan's first target. He was going for the M-16/M-203 combination rifle and grenade launcher. The deadly launcher was a weapon that would make all the difference against the Executioner, still on his back and trapped between the fallen tree trunks. He was a sitting target for a 40 mm bomb, and the Kevlar vest would only insure that the bloody stump of his torso would remain in one piece after his head, arms and legs were torn free by the detonation.

Bolan triggered his Uzi, catching the diving gunman in the center of his back. The impacts were enough to make the mercenary tumble to the ground, overshooting the powerful weapon and skidding past it. The other gunman opened fire again, raking the logs with 5.56 mm rifle rounds. Bolan curled his legs up to his chest, barely avoiding having his shins and knees chopped by the incoming bullets.

The fallen mercenary scrambled to his feet and swung his weapon around to target the Executioner. Bolan slapped both arms into the ground and rolled himself backward over his tucked head and shoulders so that he landed on his chest. Prone, the Executioner brought both hands to the Uzi, the front sight meeting the gunman's head, obscuring it.

In that instant, Bolan triggered the submachine gun. The salvo of 9 mm rounds tore out of the stubby barrel of the Uzi and made a connection between the Executioner and his target. The burst struck home, catching the enemy gunman before his bullets could come close to Bolan's form.

One last mercenary remained, armed to the teeth and covered in protective body armor.

Out of nowhere a screaming form crashed down on the Executioner's back. A fist hammered into the back of Bolan's head and drove his face into the thick bed of crushed leaves where he was nestled. The warrior surged before another blow could rain down, shrugging off the man on his back. With a half pivot, he swung his elbow hard into the stomach of a Yakuza gunman who was holding a large-framed revolver by its barrel. The Japanese mobster had to have run out of ammunition in the gunfight, but took advantage of a lull in the shooting.

Bolan wondered briefly what the hell happened to Honey, as an unknown number of Yazuka descended on them. However, those thoughts were pushed to the back of his mind as he launched his body like a missile at the Japanese gangster. The Executioner struck the man in the chest and plowed him backward over the tree trunk.

A chattering blast of automatic fire chopped the air, just missing Bolan's hurtling form as he and his opponent hit the ground with a bone-jarring thud. The soldier snapped a hard punch under the ribs of the Yakuza fighter, knocking the wind out of him for a brief moment. He lashed up with the frame of his Uzi, striking a blow that tore open the cheek and forehead of the gangster. The man went limp, and Bolan looked back.

The one surviving mercenary growled and tracked him with his rifle.

The Executioner rolled sideways, his Kevlar armor flapping over his shoulders. He sailed under a second sputtering blast of autofire as his Uzi homed in on the enemy killer. Bolan's burst struck home, but hit the gunman in his forearm and chest.

The mercenary howled in agony, dropping his assault rifle. The gunman clutched at his shattered left arm and squirmed up the hill, falling out of Bolan's sights before the Executioner could fire a follow-up burst.

Bolan hoped the gun-for-hire would realize that continuing the battle was a worthless risk of his life. The Executioner had already proved a costly enemy. Further conflict on the mercenary's part, with his shattered arm, would be suicidal.

The Executioner heard the crunch of leaves to his right and spun to face two Yakuza thugs charging at him, swinging empty rifles and shotguns like clubs. Bolan triggered the Uzi at the shotgun-toting killer and 9 mm slugs tore open the Japanese man's belly in a spray of hot blood that spattered all three of the men.

The man swinging a bolt-action rifle connected with Bolan's bicep. The impact numbed the Executioner's grip on his weapon and he dropped it to the forest floor. There was no time to draw another weapon as the Yakuza man swung his rifle around. Instead, Bolan lunged for the rifle, wrapping his big hands around the buttstock and stopping the second chop cold.

The smaller man proved to be strong and ferocious, holding on to his weapon with both hands. The Japanese gangster's face split into a snarl of feral rage as he fought to hold on to his empty weapon. Rather than trying to wrest the weapon completely from the man's hands, Bolan snapped out his foot, catching the guy in the knee. Bone cracked with the impact, and the mobster stumbled momentarily.

All the Executioner needed was that brief loss of leverage. With a savage pull, Bolan yanked the Japanese man toward him, twisting around the gunman while still holding on to the length of the hunting rifle. The weapon that was going to be used as a club to smash in the Executioner's brains was now suddenly turned into a crossbar, an implacable length of wood and steel that pressed savagely against the throat of the mobster. Panic filled the smaller man and he thrashed violently in Bolan's grasp.

The Yakuza fighter kicked his legs up, pulling his weight forward, but Bolan braced himself with a step and wrenched back tightly on the bolt-action rifle. Bolan's forearms protested at the sudden pressure, force of gravity and the Japanese gangster's straining muscles. With a lurch, the Executioner swung the body of the smaller man around. A sudden snap and the struggles of the mobster ended, his neck broken by the leverage of the steel barrel.

Bolan dropped the would-be killer to the ground and looked around, pulling the Walther from its holster.

He saw two struggling figures drop into view. One of the Yakuza gangsters was wrestling with Honey, her purple streaked blond hair flying wildly in the late-afternoon sunshine. Bolan raised his pistol to put a bullet into the Japanese mobster, but held his fire for fear of hitting Honey.

A bullet slammed into the Executioner's back before he could do another thing. The slug impacted on the flopping Kevlar vest that hung on his chest only by the shoulder straps. While it didn't provide complete protection from the hit, it did keep the 9 mm slug from penetrating Bolan's rib cage.

Staggered, Bolan turned in time to see the wounded mercenary charge. The gunman's face was contorted in fury, blind rage driving the man like a rocket toward the Executioner. Other gunshots zipped wildly past Bolan as he turned, the running mercenary's accuracy ruined by his violent motion.

The crazed man's gun ran dry before he was an arm's length away from his adversary. The Executioner pivoted on one heel, swinging his other foot into the ribs of the gunman.

The loose leaves gave way under Bolan's weight, stealing part of the force of the kick, but he still had enough power to knock the shooter sideways. The man dropped onto his injured arm and screamed in agony.

Bolan pointed the Walther at the wounded man's face. He pulled the trigger twice, killing the man instantly. He turned back to see the Yakuza mobster throw Honey to the ground. Her shotgun was in the gangster's hands, and he was hurriedly thumbing shells into the breech.

Bolan swung his pistol and punched holes in the gangster's chest with three quick shots. The mobster was thrown back by the impacts, Honey's shotgun sailing through the air as he tumbled.

"Honey!"

She looked up at Bolan, eyes wide with fear.

"Are you okay?"

She coughed and struggled to sit up.

Bolan ran to her side, checking on her.

Honey smiled weakly. Her lip was bleeding, but the piercings constricted the swelling for a moment. "Let's get the hell out of here," she said angrily.

Bolan turned and looked back at the fallen enemy mercenaries. Black shadows appeared around the bend in the gully. He spun to face Honey but saw more men in black, carrying a mix of automatic rifles and martial arts weapons.

The Burakku Uwibami cultists had waited for the end of the battle between Bolan and the others to make their move.

The Executioner was stuck with only a half-full pistol, an unfastened Kevlar vest and a stunned girl on the ground.

Implacable faces glared at Bolan, daring him to make a foolish move.

Instead, the Executioner dropped his pistol and put his hands behind his head.

**8**

Rebecca Anthony looked up at the big man, her heart sinking as she realized that the gunmen surrounding them were the cultists, men with no black market weaponry aspirations, no desire to kidnap a young woman and ransom her for money and missile plans. She swallowed hard as Cooper looked down at her, his fingers laced behind his head. She could see the momentary defeat weighing down his craggy, solemn features.

"Matt?" she asked softly.

"We'll bide our time, Honey," he answered. "Let's just do what they say. You'll have to translate for me."

Her throat tightened, tears stinging. Panic poised in the back of her mind, waiting for weakness.

"Get up, Honey," he whispered. "I'm not leaving you alone with these men. I'm not going to risk your life, either."

She staggered uneasily to her feet, looking around at the black-clad cultists. The unwavering muzzles of their barrels were as black as their ferocious eyes. Her upper teeth clicked against the twin piercings in her lower lip as she tucked them into her mouth. Cooper stood protectively by her side, even though he could really do nothing.

He'd shown himself to be an amazing warrior of remarkable skill, but without any weapons in hand, and so many killers aiming their guns at him, there was nothing he could do but stand still and behave. She blamed herself. If she hadn't been knocked onto her ass, disarmed by the Yakuza gunman, he wouldn't have had to race to her rescue with a half-empty pistol. Because of her, he was unarmed and unable to lead them to escape. Her fists clenched at her sides as she looked warily at the men around him.

"Just put your hands behind your head, Honey," Bolan said. "They think you're going to try to fight."

"I let us down."

"No, you didn't," he answered. "You held up the Yakuza men long enough for me to take care of them."

"Enough talking!" one of the cultists said in English. "Give me your hands!"

Honey glanced over to Bolan, uncertain. He nodded his approval.

She presented her wrists, and the cultist stepped forward with a length of cord. He was quick, efficient, but rough with the lashings, binding her hands together. He tugged and pulled her, but didn't pull the cord tight enough to dig into her flesh though she couldn't get any leverage or slack to pull free. She could tell that right away.

"You next," the Black Serpent ordered Bolan. "Any moves…she dies!"

The big American narrowed his eyes and lowered his hands, outstretched. Two of the Japanese cultists rushed up from behind, and Honey could see Cooper tense at their approach, fighting against a conditioned reflex to protect himself. Gun barrels flipped under his loosely hanging Kevlar vest, pressing into the bare flesh of his torso. The stab of the submachine guns against his ribs forced him to take a step forward, and the man who tied Honey's hands whipped out a knife. The arc of the blade stopped just short of the Executioner's Adam's apple.

Bolan didn't flinch at the presence of unyielding steel.

"I said no moves!" the spokesman for the group said.

Bolan simply nodded in understanding, the sharp edge of steel scraping a raw red spot on his throat.

Honey winced at the sight, and regarded their situation.

At least being held captive by the mercenaries or the Yakuza, she knew that she had protection, that she'd be kept alive as long as someone was willing to pay for her. With these madmen, things were even more bleak. Cooper had explained to her that they were cultural isolationists, and they hated the advances of the west, intrusions on their soil. Honey, in her Goth finery, was an open sore in their eyes, an American corruptor of the youth of Japan.

She bit back a whimper, once again blaming herself. If she hadn't come to Japan, she wouldn't have proved such a tasty target to entrepenurial Japanese gangsters. This nightmare could have been avoided if she'd gone somewhere where her father would have arranged protection for her, instead of using his money to get as far away from him as she could.

The belle-of-the-ball look was discarded for midnight black vestments and ripped lace. Leather pumps were thrown away for combat boots. Her rose petal lips were pierced with gleaming steel rings and painted black. Her blue eyes were set in hollows of murky dark eye shadow, and her blond curly hair was greasy flat and streaked with grape Kool-Aid. As much as she tried to peel away the existence of her father in her life, she was still a product of his money, and a victim of his world of multimillion dollar arms trades and international intrigue.

As far as she tried to run, even when she slipped his protection, his shadow loomed over her. And this time, she'd dragged a man to his doom with her.

She watched as the cord was yanked taut around Cooper's

wrists, its black length digging into his tanned forearms. He clenched his wrists, but the knife was back at his throat.

"Relax your wrists!" the cultist ordered. "Relax them now!"

Cooper stared at him for a moment, testing the limits of the man's patience before letting his muscles grow slack.

Cooper remained silent as the cord was pulled tight around his flesh. It took longer for them to tie him up than it did for Honey, but she knew that was because they considered him the greater threat. They were taking into account his greater size and obvious strength.

While Honey couldn't tell how old Cooper was, he had a body that most athletes would have envied. His bare arms were tautly muscled, corded tightly around the bones. When he moved, his limbs swelled with power, rippling with a strength that she knew didn't come from hours on some exercise machine. His was the body of a man who tested himself to the limits on a regular basis.

Cooper caught her looking at him and nodded again to her. Each time he did so, things seemed to be right. Even surrounded by eight hostile enemies, she knew that she was as safe as she could be, just for his presence. If there was a way out of this nightmare, he would be the one to guide her there.

Honey had nothing to fear, she suddenly realized. If anything, she felt a sort of fiendish glee, anticipating the world of hurt that the Black Serpents were going to inherit.

Matt Cooper may have been captured, but she was confident he would not be held for long.

HOGAN AND MACHIDA RACED at the head of their ragged, battered little group. Freshly laden with borrowed weapons and ammunition, they were charging toward the last position that Nickles had radioed from. They hadn't been far from his location, maybe less than a half mile away, a trip made longer by the thickness of the woods, hills and ruts that ran along the wrinkled floor of the valley.

The sounds of gunfire and grenades spurred the mercenaries and Yakuza men to run faster. Conflict had broken out and they didn't want to miss out and leave their only surviving backup without assistance.

The gunfire ended as swiftly as it began, and Hogan slowed up their formation.

"Should we not hurry?" Machida asked.

"I don't like this at all," Hogan said. "I just tried contacting Nickles over my throat mike."

"No response?" Machida asked.

"No. He would have at least given an empty click in reply to my inquiry," Hogan said.

Machida looked down. "They were defeated."

"That bastard Cooper has been killing too many of my men," Hogan snarled.

"Perhaps it was the others," Machida offered.

"No. We've been able to handle these local chokers," Hogan said. "But this guy Cooper, he's been a thorn in my side since I left Tokyo."

"You tried to eliminate him and failed. Twice."

"We were too cramped up in the van," Hogan explained. "And then, one of my men underestimated Cooper and let him sneak up on him."

"Making excuses is unbecoming," Machida said.

Hogan whirled, pointing his finger into the Yakuza man's face. "Listen, pal. I'm just saying this Cooper guy is good enough that he made me regret taking him as a lightweight. But we're not going to underestimate him again."

"Remove your finger from my face."

"You're lucky we need each other," Hogan growled.

"I do not call this luck," Machida answered. "I call this, at best, karmic punishment for having brought our business to this damned stretch of woods."

Hogan sneered. "Then maybe you should get out of the girl-kidnapping business if you're so afraid that instant karma is gonna get you."

"Enough," Machida snapped back. "We have come looking for the Anthony girl. Once we have her, we'll go about our business and escape this viper's nest."

Hogan smirked. "You just love being right, don't you?"

"It's not a matter of getting into what you call a pissing contest," Machida responded. "It's simple pragmatism. If we go at each other's throats now, we'll only bring down our pursuers on us, and when they find the victor, whomever is left will be weakened and outnumbered enough that they too will die."

Hogan shook his head, grumbling under his breath.

"You're right," he finally conceded.

Machida led the group, in a crouch, to the top of the hill and stopped, spotting movement below. He ducked even lower, laying on his chest. Hogan slithered to his side, his reptilian eyes slits in his face.

"Looks like Cooper's finally run into our welcoming committee," Hogan whispered.

"They're taking the guns off the dead men," Machida noted, nodding toward the Black Serpents who were policing their fallen comrades.

"So?" Hogan asked.

"Perhaps their resources are not as all encompassing as we once thought," Machida explained.

Hogan nodded. "We're not sure how many of them are here in this valley. But, they have body armor and automatic weapons."

Hogan brought his binoculars to his eyes and scanned the scene. "They're definitely taking both Cooper and Anthony hostage. Tied them both up. And they ain't taking any chances with Cooper. They put a knife to his throat twice and have two guns poked in his back."

Machida squinted, trying to get a better look at the girl. From this distance, all he could see was her wild tangle of purple-streaked blond hair. "They've only tied them up? The girl looks as if she has been in a fight."

"There's a bruise on her jaw and she's got a shiner starting to form," Hogan told him. "But it doesn't look like these guys did it."

Machida looked at the scene. All of the mercenaries were strewed along one side of the narrow rut, their bodies torn by submachine gun fire. On the other side, his Yakuza men were more spread out, in varying degrees of distance between the top of the hill and where Cooper and Honey were standing. That meant it was his men who went after her. They had roughed her up.

A deep shame rushed through Machida.

He admired the young woman. She was willing to risk a bullet in order to achieve her own freedom, on her own terms. She might have started out annoying, one of the tragically hip Goth types that marked themselves as outsiders to society, but even that endeared the girl to him. Her piercings were as much a badge of her own station as the tattoos across his back and down his arms.

He felt a kinship with the girl.

Machida's respect extended to Agent Matt Cooper. The ferocity with which he protected the girl, fending off ten-to-one odds, going from unarmed fugitive to having proved a match for automatic-weapon-armed mercenaries was astounding. Machida didn't know where the submachine gun that Cooper had used came from, but he suspected that not only had the FBI agent battled Hogan's mercenaries and his own Yakuza foot soldiers, but he had probably encountered some of the black-clad mystery commandos who inhabited this valley.

Men whom Machida himself had faced in combat and knew to be deadly and efficient.

Whoever this Cooper was, he was a formidable warrior, and one who showed a dedication that would have put even the Yakuza's finest to shame. He stayed by the girl's side, protective of her despite his own relative helplessness.

Machida felt no doubt that given an opportunity, Cooper would get Honey to freedom himself.

Machida had a sudden idea.

"Let's follow them," he told Hogan.

"What?"

"We should follow them. When the mystery men get reckless, we'll move in and attack," Machida told Hogan. "Otherwise, we'll lose Honey."

Hogan glanced at the scene and nodded. "Yeah. Those guys are too uptight right now. If we make a move, they'll hold down the trigger and smoke anything that moves."

Machida felt some vindication as Hogan recognized the wisdom of his plan. "If we follow them, we'll be able to determine the location of their headquarters. We can grab Cooper and Honey, and retreat. Once we know where they're located, then we can sneak back and appropriate one of their vehicles to get out of here."

"Good idea," Hogan stated. He made a fist and circled it in the air. The other mercenaries closed in. Machida's men followed the signal as well.

Hogan handed Machida the binoculars, and the Yakuza boss turned and observed the group of cultists as they surrounded Honey and Cooper. He scanned her first, and sure enough, she showed signs of rough treatment. He clenched his teeth and studied Cooper next.

Tall, powerful, leanly built with a hard, craggy face with ice-blue eyes that pierced everything they looked upon as if he were seeing through the skin and flesh, deep into the hearts and minds of the men around him. He was probing, reaching, searching for weaknesses and filing them away for future reference.

If they attacked as Machida had suggested, then Cooper would leap on the opportunity and disappear like smoke.

Machida moved his glasses around and saw Unno, recognizing his clothes and his long hair. Unno lay on the ground, his face a bloody mess, long strands of black hair matted to his flesh. A mixture of regret and reproach churned in Machida's gut over the death of Unno. Then he saw the man's foot move. He was still breathing, but the horrible mask of crimson matting his face disguised his true condition.

He lowered his binoculars.

"I see that one of my men survived. If the cultists don't notice him, he may make it through," Machida explained. "We can get more information about them."

"And even up the sides between your men and mine," Hogan said.

Machida handed the binoculars back to Hogan, who slipped them around his neck. The mercenary boss wasn't happy.

It didn't matter to Machida. Let Hogan be furious with him. As long as they were outnumbered, there was no way they could risk losing even one potential ally.

But Hogan's suspicions were correct. Machida did want to stand on equal footing with the mercenary. It was already too late to get any advantage on the American hard case. But Machida vowed one thing to himself.

Reckoning was coming for the soldier of fortune.

BOLAN CAUGHT THE GLINT of the binoculars out of the corner of his eye as he surveyed the Burakku Uwibami cultists around him. The scene was becoming crowded, but when no bullet screamed through his head, he knew that Hogan and Machida weren't in any condition to take on a dozen alert and hostile commandos.

Bolan decided he would keep this information to himself. There was too much of a risk that their captors would catch even a slight hand gesture. If they figured out that someone was going to try to take away their prize, Bolan's and Honey's lives would be forfeit.

The Executioner had battled too long and too hard to let a simple mistake take the girl's chances of survival away.

"Move!" the English-speaking cultist ordered. He'd switched from a knife to his machine pistol, keeping its muzzle aimed at the tall American warrior.

Bolan obeyed. He knew from experience that following orders, no matter how humiliating or degrading, was the best tactic when held at gunpoint. Trying the patience of an armed madman was tantamount to suicide. Honey squirmed as one of the other cultists shoved her.

Bolan shook his head and nodded for her to follow him. Honey's mouth drew into a tight line. The swelling of her lower lip was increasing, and blood trickled down her chin, staining it red. The constriction of her lip piercings had to have been agonizing, but she suffered quietly.

She wasn't a trained warrior like he was, but she showed a strength, an iron resolve that Bolan couldn't help but appreciate.

It would take every bit of Bolan's ability to make sure that she'd be safe. He heard the beeping of a cell phone and turned his head.

Someone was reporting in, and that would mean that they would be made aware of the presence of the mercenary-Yakuza combined force. But Bolan knew if he tried to interrupt the call, he'd be cut to ribbons. The spokesman rattled off a quick phrase in Japanese.

Bolan glanced to Honey, who was listening intently. Her blue eyes met his for an instant, and she nodded slightly.

Honey's shoulders tensed as she listened to the phone conversation, and Bolan wondered what was going through her mind.

MACHIDA LOWERED his glasses as he saw Honey look directly at him. She was squinting in his direction. She looked toward him the moment the cultist holding her started speaking on the phone. That meant that the men below knew they were being watched. Machida didn't know how—they'd been as stealthy as snakes.

Someone else was watching them. He looked around slowly, but no one was shadowing their group. Machida guessed that somewhere in the valley, there was an array of sensors. Maybe microwave fences, or seismic motion detectors. Whatever it was, their element of surprise was all but blown.

Machida's doubts suddenly crystalized into a flash of confidence.

He knew that the enemy was aware of their presence. Hogan and his mercenaries did not. Suddenly he had an advantage over Hogan.

All he had to do was make sure that Hogan made the first move, and then he'd fade back, letting Hogan's men take the heat from the black-clad guardians of the valley. In that instant, the Yakuza men would be able to fall back and elude their enemy, knowing full well that they were under electronic surveillance. Cooper would make his escape with Honey, and Machida would be alive to try to get her back.

If he played his cards right, he could even throw in with the American specialist, get him to assist them against the hostile locals.

All he needed was for those bastards to move and let them get to Unno, before he sat up and got himself killed.

UNNO HEARD THE SOUNDS of feet crushing leaves and grass, and the voice of strangers speaking Japanese. The last thing he could remember was the crash of steel against his face, and though he was huring, he didn't move, didn't make a sound. He kept his breath flat and even. His chest didn't rise or fall.

Playing dead was going to keep him alive.

Finally, the voices stopped. They were speaking English, probably to prisoners. That meant the Americans had survived.

Unno stayed still. From what he could understand of their chatter, the enemy knew that someone was following them, shadowing them. Unno knew that it had to be Machida, and maybe that bastard Hogan.

The men around him finally left. Unno could tell by the sounds of footsteps and lack of breathing that the enemy were moving away, and he slitted his eye open a fraction of an inch.

Silence reigned. He was alone in the gully.

"Unno," came a whisper.

It was Machida's voice. He didn't move.

"Unno, are you okay?" Machida asked, kneeling beside the battered Yakuza man.

"I'm alive, but my face feels as if it were on fire," Unno answered.

"In English, so the rest of us jokers can understand," Hogan growled.

Unno sat up slowly. He eyed the American mercenary.

"I said," Unno shouted, "it feels as if my face were on fire."

Hogan shook his head. "Jonas, take care of this guy's face fast. We don't want to lose the Anthony girl."

The man with the medical kit nodded and immediately began working on Unno's face.

Machida met Unno's angry gaze and nodded to him. Unno realized that his boss had something up his sleeve, and Unno nodded, too quickly for the mercenaries to catch it. Unno had faith in the Yakuza leader. He'd pulled miracles out of his hat before.

# 9

Bolan felt prickling and tingling in his hands as the cords around his wrists cut off his circulation. He did his best to angle his arms in front of him to get fresh rushes of blood into his fingers so he wouldn't suffer later. By clenching his fists and unflexing them, he found that he was able to get a flow of warmth back into his cooling, darkening hands, enough to prevent permanent damage. The flesh on his wrists was raw and as the top layer of dermis peeled away with the rough gouging of the cord binding him, he began to bleed.

Bolan didn't want to do too much in loosening his bindings. He didn't want it to seem like he was escaping. He knew that any misstep, any attempt to move without a proper distraction, would mean death.

The Executioner knew he couldn't risk anything that could lead to harming his innocent companion.

The Black Serpents were just another group of soulless predators who needed crushing under foot. Bolan had battled figurative serpents of all kinds across his long career. His sword hand was steady, confident and capable.

If only I had a sword with me, he thought. He'd stashed one away, along with a trio of pistols and a handful of other martial-arts gear that he knew would be too much to carry while surviving the trek through the valley. Having a backup stash of supplies hadn't been his goal in hiding the leftovers from the dead Black Serpents, it was just a weight saving exercise. But, he knew where that was, and how to backtrack to that site. All he needed was the right opportunity. It was only a couple of guns and handheld melee weapons. Against men with body armor and automatic weapons, Bolan would be severely outgunned as well as outnumbered.

Bolan frowned. Honey wasn't looking at him. He could see the look on her face; she was furious.

Bolan knew a lot of that anger was directed at him, but not all of it. He'd told her that he'd keep her from being taken captive again. But when it came down to a choice between dying free and living a little longer in captivity, Bolan chose life. There was always the possibility of escape. While Honey wasn't happy to be tied up and forced into a march, she kept going, not pushing her luck against the cultists. That meant she knew there was a chance of getting out of this alive, and she was keeping her head. She turned and looked at him, a mixture of fierce determination and uncertaintly fighting for control of her face. She closed her eyes for a moment and looked away, paying attention to the path in front of her instead.

Bolan remembered his decision to test the waters by allowing himself to stumble and lose his balance when the march began. His back ached with fresh bruises, and his mangled shoulder was bleeding down his back again, after the cultists flew into a rage, smashing him with the butts of their guns. He was still woozy from the beating, but that was all the information he or Honey needed. If they fell, they'd be battered until they got back to their feet.

It was a costly lesson, and Bolan knew the reopened lashes in his shoulder were draining away vital blood and moisture. The cultists were not likely to give him any fresh water, even when they threw him in a cell. Dehydration was an all too real danger. He felt parched already, and he knew from experience that things would get far worse.

As far as Bolan could tell, they were nearing a sheer cliff that formed the western border of the valley. The cliff was hundreds of feet high, and while outcroppings sported sparse bushes and grasses, it was dark and imposing now that the sun had dipped behind it. They were in its shadow already, and the cultists had slowed, no longer keeping a frantic pace. They whispered among themselves, and Bolan figured that they were nearing their headquarters.

And getting this close, they were allowing themselves to become more attractive as bait for Hogan and Machida, who were undoubtedly still following them. Bolan wondered if the remaining mercenaries and Yakuza gunmen were aware that they were following him into a trap, but he didn't care either way. As long as Hogan and Machida made their move, then the Executioner could take his opportunity and get Honey out of there.

Bolan flexed and released his fists again, once more giving his hands a fresh supply of blood. The cords were now cutting deep into his skin, splitting the surface and slicking his wrists with a patina of dark crimson. Getting out of his bindings would be a top priority, but getting some space between himself and the cult gunmen was the first goal on his list. As he flexed and released his fists, he kept his senses alert.

It would be a matter of timing. Split seconds would decide whether Bolan and Honey survived or not. He scanned the sides of their trail, looking for paths that provide cover for them. Escape routes, arcs of fire, reaction times, all were plotting through his mind.

That was the key to the Executioner's survival. Not by being a good shot, not by being strong, not by having the biggest guns—it was having a mind as sharp as a razor, and constantly keeping it in motion, like a shark on the hunt, always awake, always sniffing for traces of weakness to pounce on.

Keenly observant, he did not miss the red dot dancing across the back of the man in the lead.

A laser sight.

Bolan looked at Honey. She wasn't ready, but he hadn't really expected her to know that they were going to get their chance. All he had to do was wait for the first shot.

The laser dot disappeared. It was just a ranging pulse, probably to give the shooter his bearings on where to aim. A smart shot would have an optical scope to verify where the laser dot landed on the target, would memorize the angle, then shut off the telltale red marker before anyone among the enemy noticed that one or more of their own were being "lit up." Hogan's men were good and smart.

Bolan was glad that he'd been able to keep one step ahead, one bullet faster than the mercenaries. He hoped they were good enough to provide the distraction he needed to escape.

The Executioner's heartbeat increased in response to his recognition of impending action. The tingling in his hands disappeared as his blood pressure rose. Oxygen was being force fed to every cell of his being. Bolan experienced the surge on an almost daily, sometimes hourly basis, given his lifestyle. The adrenaline was surging.

The Executioner would be able to perform that much faster, simply because he was used to operating under pressure. Instead of becoming fumble fingered and nervous with the rush of the endorphins in his bloodstream, he had long ago become used to it and was able to tune himself to maximum effect. Even the bite of the cords into his muscled wrists was no longer as sharp and painful.

The path made a bend and they rounded it. As they did,

Bolan could see a small compound ahead, behind a fence overgrown with ivy. Camouflage netting covered buildings and tents, breaking up their outline from the air, and the Executioner memorized as much of the layout as he could see in that one instant, before continuing to gauge the approach of Hogan and the Yazuka, and his own escape path.

Bolan could imagine, as he plotted the mercenaries and Yakuza's approach to the Black Serpents, their sudden impression of the sprawling, yet camouflaged base hidden ahead of them. Suddenly, the whole situation had altered for the ragtag gunmen and mobsters, and they were facing a well-organized, heavily fortified enemy force. It would be enough to give them pause. Indeed, Bolan himself was impressed with the fortress in the shadow of the cliff.

But his awe at the resources of his enemy didn't keep his mind pinned down, not when he had plans racing through his brain, a terrain map altering with each footstep forward. He held his breath as they continued around the bend, heading on the final straightaway to the painted chain link front gate.

It was now or never.

Come on, Hogan, he thought.

The first gunshot came not as a shock, but a body-warming relief, the bullet smashing the back of the English-speaking cultist's head open. Black hair and red chunks of skull flew in all directions, the man's body jerking forward with the force of the lethal impact. In one fluid motion, Bolan whirled and wrapped his hands around Honey's forearm. Going for a weapon would have given him the chance to shoot back, but that would have left the girl standing still too long in the middle of a firefight.

She was his priority. He hauled her as if she were a pillow, lifting her off her feet. One of her loafers flew from a bandaged foot, but there was no time to stop and go back for it. Instead, Bolan hauled her to the side of the trail, dragging them both through the grasses and bushes as the flurry of gunfire behind him erupted to thunderous life, snapping and crackling like a storm.

Honey was screaming as the Executioner yanked her along, her feet slipping as she pumped her legs to keep up with him. She didn't fall—he held on to her too tightly, and his footing was far more certain. A dull numbness warmed its way through his back and one part of his mind focused on it, evaluating the sensation. Already his hips were moving more stiffly as he ran, and he wondered how badly he'd pulled his back muscles, but still, he plowed on, boots crushing foliage and snapping twigs beneath their soles.

A single bullet sliced through the woods, caroming off Bolan's left bicep, nicking the skin before disappearing into the shadowy forest. The Executioner felt barely more than a minor sting, despite the rivulets of blood.

"Slow down!" Honey howled, and she slipped once more. She nearly yanked Bolan off balance, but with a surge of strength, he dragged her back up to her feet.

A figure in black darted through the forest, shouting at them in Japanese and the Executioner twisted and threw himself on top of Honey. She let out an explosive breath as he fell, covering her. Above them, gunfire slashed the air, tearing apart a tree trunk.

The Japanese man continued to rush forward, but he was clumsily trying to reload his weapon. Bolan lurched to his feet, his ice-cold eyes locking on his target even as the man closed on them. The black-clad attacker froze as he saw the bound Executioner rise before him, then pounce at him, both hands clamping down on his empty submachine gun. The Black Serpent ambusher cursed in Japanese as he tried to maintain a hold on his weapon, but the steel frame of the gun popped free from his grip.

Bolan had an empty hunk of metal in his hands, and the cultist reached down, flipping free a *kami* sickle. A simple farm tool pressed into service as a martial arts weapon, the *kami* was a foot-long length of wood with a wicked, curved blade swooping out of one end. Even in inexpert hands, the sickle would cause heinous injuries, carving easily into soft, unprotected flesh.

The sickle-man swept up his weapon and lashed down brutally with the lethal blade. Bolan pivoted and swung the frame of the submachine gun. Steel barked on steel in a blow that sent tremors rumbling up Bolan's forearms. The Japanese killer bounced back from the first swing, surprised at the American's deft defense. He'd left himself open for Bolan's slashing kick. Breath exploded from the cultist's lungs with the brutal impact, and the big American stepped forward, hammering the frame of the submachine gun against the side of his opponent's head.

The black-clad man staggered, and Bolan chopped down again, catching him at the crook of the neck with six pounds of steel. Almost too late, the American warrior backed away from the deadly arc of the *kami*, its point dragging along his ribs. He received a long, bloody, but shallow scratch. Bolan spun on one heel and swung the empty submachine gun at the sickle-wielding killer. Steel met flesh and bone, the Executioner's strike hitting the cultist's rib cage.

With a quick flip and change of direction, Bolan yanked up his improvised club, catching his enemy under the chin. The attacker flopped backward, crashing to the forest floor like a felled tree. Bolan knew his opponent wasn't finished yet. Leaping forward, he straddled the man's chest and chopped down, crunching bone with one final skull smashing swing.

Honey was coughing, staggering to all fours, and Bolan grabbed the *kami*, bringing the sharp edge down to the cords around his wrists, sawing as fast as he could. The blade bit into the bindings hungrily, parting the restraints with little effort. With a savage shake, Bolan pulled himself free, the cords reluctantly releasing their deep grip on his flesh, blood flowing freely from where they had cut his skin.

"Honey," Bolan snarled, turning with the *kami* in one hand. He grabbed one of her forearms and pulled her forward, slicing down with the razor-sharp blade. It took less time for her to get her free, since both of his hands were loose and able to move.

"I need to catch my breath," Honey began, but fresh gunfire and the sudden flash of a figure in black approaching them forced Bolan to yank her to her feet once again. Still gripping the sickle in one fist, pulling the girl along by her arm, the Executioner was on the move.

There simply had not been enough time to find the submachine gun, its spare magazines and reload the weapon. Not with enemies breaking off into the forest, pursuing them at full speed. This was their territory, and they knew it, probably to the location of every tree. Honey scrambled, her feet slipping on the leaf-covered forest floor, but she pumped along, cursing each time her bloody, bandaged foot struck the ground.

Better to curse than to utter a death cry, Bolan thought.

"Keep moving!" Bolan yelled to her. Even hobbled as she was, Honey had no choice but to keep up, her shorter strides frantically attempting match the fleeing Executioner.

The tree line broke in front of them, and Bolan skidded to a halt, inches from the edge of another cliff, twenty feet high, looking down over a murky, deep section of river. Honey didn't quite stop. Her feet slipped off the edge and sailed into space. The Executioner's arm strained to hold up her weight and stop her momentum, his legs bracing against her mass as he hauled her back into his arms.

A blast of bullets let Bolan know that the enemy was still close behind them.

"Can you swim?" Bolan asked.

"What?" Honey was confused, totally lost. Things were happening too fast for her to process.

Bolan would have to take his chances. He lurched forward, clutching the girl tight against his chest. Honey suddenly realized they were falling and let out a wail of surprise. More gunfire chased them over the edge, but gravity sucked the two people back to Earth's embrace. Water enveloped the Executioner and the girl as they plunged.

HOGAN'S MEN HAD FINALLY begun the ambush of the men holding Cooper and the Anthony girl hostage. Machida fired off a couple of short bursts toward the armed enemy, taking care not to hit either of the Americans with his submachine gun.

The return fire was swift and furious, and one of Machida's own soldiers was swatted by a wall of lead that chopped him to pieces. Unno growled and scooped up the dead man's SMG, firing back at the line of men in the clearing.

Machida watched as Cooper yanked the Anthony girl off her feet, disappearing behind the trees in a flash of fluid motion that confirmed the Yakuza leader's assessment of his skill. No doubt that Cooper and the girl would be gone within moments, far beyond the reach of the mysterious defenders of the forest, as well as Hogan and his own forces.

Machida grabbed Unno's shoulder and nodded for him to follow. The surviving Yakuza gunmen all whirled as one, tearing off into the woods as the rattle of automatic fire ripped the air apart behind them.

"I thought we wanted to get the girl!" Unno said as they ran.

"She's getting away. We can always find her later," Machida told him. "Did you hear if these strangers knew about us?"

"Yeah," Unno answered. "The goons who grabbed the Americans were talking about being shadowed."

Machida leaped over a log and landed on the other side, not even breaking his stride as he continued retreating into the forest. "That means they must have some kind of sensors."

"Could be. They didn't say," Unno replied. "We're leaving the mercenaries behind?"

"It was time to cut our losses and run," Machida answered.

"What about the plans?" Unno asked. "The blueprints we were supposed to get."

"Hopefully these forest raiders haven't gone through Hogan's vehicles," Machida told him. "We can find the blueprints and leave."

"And if not?" Unno asked.

"We have backup coming," Machida told him. "And we're going to get the Anthony girl back."

Unno managed a smirk through his bandaged features. "Sounds like a good plan, boss."

"We'll find out soon enough," Machida said.

HOGAN SAW THAT the Yakuza men had disappeared. He snarled and fired another burst at the group of black-clad cultists on the path, his line of fire decapitating one of the Japanese with an explosive display of 9 mm slugs.

"Shit! Something's up!" Hogan shouted. "Pull back!"

One of his mercenaries rose to begin the retreat when suddenly he was stopped, pierced through the chest with the point of a spear. Throughout the woods around them, dark figures lurched from the trees, wielding a mix of modern and ancient weapons. Hogan knew what these guys had managed to do to Machida's gangsters in the battle at the graveyard. The bastards had drawn them into another trap.

Hogan plucked a grenade from his harness and hurled it, striking a sword-wielding ambusher in the chest. A heartbeat later, the minibomb detonated, tossing the raggedy corpse away as if it were a doll. Shooting from the hip and on the run, the mercenary leader wasn't firing for effect, only to keep heads down while he broke through the line of ambushers.

Surrounded and outnumbered, there was no way he was going to stand his ground and fight to the last. As it was, only one other of his men was hot on his heels as they raced through the opening that Hogan had made in the attackers. Bulling through saplings and bushes, his pace never slackened as he and his sole surviving mercenary ally charged toward freedom.

Hogan's last man threw a pair of grenades behind him, lobbing them both at once, and continued his mad run. Hogan himself felt the impact of a bullet bounce off his Kevlar-protected shoulder. He was getting plenty damn sick and tired of getting hammered on this little operation, but he didn't stop to fire a burst in revenge for the shot.

He just kept on racing to freedom, as if all the serpents in hell were at his back.

Static burst over his earphone. It was Sinclair's voice.

"Hogan! What the hell is going on?" he asked.

"No time to talk! Can you track me?"

"We're right above you," Sinclair answered. "There's a clearing about twenty-five yards ahead of you. Keep going straight."

Hogan didn't have to be told twice. The mercenary behind

him also heard and poured on the speed, but stumbled, screaming as a blade sank into his neck.

Hogan glanced back, seeing his man tumble to the ground in a sprawl of limbs, struggling to get back to his feet. Black-clad figures fell upon him, not killing him, but grappling with him, hauling him deeper into the woods, presumably back toward the encampment at the base of the cliff.

Hogan winced, wished the poor bastard luck and continued charging on. Just because some of the enemy had stopped to grab his last remaining trooper didn't mean that the others had given up their pursuit of him.

Within moments, Hogan burst into the clearing, where three helicopters were hovering over the scene. He continued running, reaching. Hurtling figures bounded from the tree line, shouting in Japanese. From the doors of two of the helicopters, M-60 machine guns spoke, ripping up the earth and punching holes in the pursuers.

The enemy retreated. Sinclair's helicopter dropped a rope ladder to him. Hogan leaped, discarding his gun and hooking his arms through the rungs. In moments, the helicopter rose into the sky, under the thundering cover fire of the machine guns.

Hogan looked back, panting heavily.

The serpents of hell at his back had just met his elite force. Just like those bastards Machida and Cooper would.

**10**

Honey Anthony broke the surface, sucking in a deep lungful of air. Her hair fell into her eyes, and she couldn't see, but she splashed on the surface.

"Matt!" she cried out.

Dammit, she cursed to herself. Quit being such a wimp! Swim for shore!

She thrashed around, then screamed as an arm snaked around her waist and hauled her back.

"Wait," Bolan growled into her ear. "It's me."

Honey panted breathlessly. "Quit doing the *Creature from the Black Lagoon* bit...."

"Quiet," Bolan said. He put his hand over her mouth for emphasis. The big American swam with her, dragging her toward the cliff. From up above, she heard voices.

Suddenly a pair of shapes dropped into the water. Honey squirmed in Bolan's grip, realizing that they hadn't escape the enemy yet. The Executioner released her and dived under the water. The men who'd jumped popped to the surface, gasping from the shock of hitting the chilled water. One looked straight at her, and Honey gulped, freezing like a deer in the headlights.

Suddenly the man looking at her gave a cry as he was dragged beneath the surface. The other man splashed frantically.

Honey clung to the side of the cliff, digging her fingers into hanging roots that jutted from the muddy face. Maybe she could climb out of this mess before that cultist could swim after her and capture her. Or worse, try to kill her.

UNDER THE MURKY SURFACE, the Executioner's hold on the cultist's belt snagged as the smaller man twisted violently, trying to pull free. A kicking leg connected with Bolan's chin and snapped his head back, bubbles of vital breath erupting from his lips with the impact. The cultist tried to swing his machine pistol around, but Bolan twisted in the water, snaking both legs around the cultist's arm, scissoring it between his powerful thighs.

Flexing his legs and wrenching his entire body around, the Executioner felt the crunch of snapping joints, and an explosion of bubbles escaping his enemy's mouth. With a mighty pull, Bolan untangled himself from the man's belt and pushed forward with the *kami*, driving the sickle's blade deep into the Black Serpent's belly. The murky brown water darkened as a cloud of blood billowed like smoke, spreading rapidly around them.

The cultist clawed at his torn stomach with one hand, but he only held on for a moment, his body going limp from shock. Bolan unwrapped his legs from around the drowning man's dislocated arm and kicked toward the surface, where another of the divers was swimming toward the cliff.

Toward Honey.

Breaking the surface, the Executioner replenished the oxygen in his lungs and saw his next target. Honey had crawled halfway out of the water. Bolan kicked forward, chopping down with the *kami*, it's wicked point snagging on something solid. The enemy swimmer cried out and twisted, glaring hatefully at the American warrior.

Good, Bolan thought, he wasn't paying attention to the girl anymore. That would give her a chance while he dealt with the cultist.

Movement at the ledge overlooking the water drew Bolan's attention. Two more cultists were standing above him. They leveled their automatic weapons, but as they were adjusting their aim, the Executioner was taking action. Slicing into the depths of the water, he dived out of the path of gunfire but continued to torpedo his way toward the swimming cultist on Honey's trail.

Reaching up, Bolan snagged an ankle and swung the sickle once more, raking its unyielding edge across the man's calf. Flesh and clothing parted under the metal's brutal assault. More blood mixed with the murky silt of the river water. The cultist twirled, trying to kick out of Bolan's grip, and managed to hammer his heel into the side of the Executioner's head. If it weren't for the resistance of the water, the stomp would have done more than bruise.

Bolan refused to let go. Hanging on, he lashed out again with the *kami*. Steel bit mercilessly into flesh, plunging deep, and the cultist bucked wildly in the Executioner's grasp. Pulling himself up on the handle of the sickle, Bolan realized that he'd stabbed the man through the groin, severing a major artery. Jets of blood merged with the water, all but blinding Bolan in a dark cloud. Wrenching the sickle free, the Executioner punched with it, striking the man in the chest with the wicked, hooked blade.

The death throes of the swimmer tore the handle from Bolan's grip, and the dead man spiraled to the riverbed below. There was no time to try to retrieve his only weapon. Bolan broke the surface and dug his fingers into the side of the cliff.

Breathing deeply, he sucked in fresh air, and noticed that Honey was perched on the face of the drop off, only the lip of the ledge keeping the two gunmen above them from seeing her.

"Where now?" Honey asked. She was soaked, and the cold bit into her flesh, making her tremble uncontrollably. Her knuckles were white as they grabbed on to protruding roots.

Bolan realized that his own body temperature was dropping from exposure to the cold water. It had only been a couple minutes but it wouldn't take long for someone in the river to develop hypothermia. Only the fact that his muscles were shot through with adrenaline and oxygen kept him from feeling the full effect of the icy chill at the moment.

More bullets chopped into the water, seeking the Executioner and his charge. Bolan snagged a root and hauled himself up, water trying to suck him back down, his tattered shirt and pants clinging to his soaking flesh. A few more handholds, a few more pulls, and he was out of the river, climbing toward Honey.

"Stay put," Bolan said.

"You don't have a gun," Honey said.

The Executioner shot her a grin. "I'm working on it."

One of the cultists on the ledge dropped into the water behind him, and Bolan twisted, kicking off with all his strength. His body stiffened into a spear, and he aimed right for the man. Bolan connected with his target, fingers clawing into the cultist's clothes, the entirety of his weight piledriving through the smaller Japanese madman. Both of their bodies sunk deep in the water, and the Executioner swung himself around.

It was none too soon, as his opponent shuddered under the impact of high-powered bullets that drilled through the water and slammed into his back. Even though the Black Serpent was wearing Kevlar, the multiple bullet strikes knocked the air out of him, driving the fight from his limbs. Bolan kicked hard, pulling them both deeper into the murky brown depths, enemy gunfire still spitting through the darkness around them.

Bolan's shield squirmed and struggled for breath, trying to tear himself free from the grip of the big hands of the American drawing him to a cold, watery demise. The Executioner let go with one hand, reaching for the machine pistol the gunman was still holding. Fingers brushed metal, and Bolan lunged desperately, wrapping his fingers around the barrel.

The Black Serpent writhed like his namesake, and one flailing hand raked across Bolan's forehead, gouging scratches into his skin. Bolan ignored the sudden sting, clutching the assault weapon with all of his strength. More gunfire chopped the surface of the water.

Finally, Bolan twisted the machine pistol free from his submerged opponent, and pushed the heavy metal frame, crashing the buttstock into the man's jaw. The blow, in open air, would have crushed bone and snapped his enemy's neck like a twig. But under the water, Bolan only managed to daze the Japanese cultist.

Bolan reversed his stroke and hammered again with the metal buttstock, stamping the steel right into the face of the Black Serpent gunman. Fingers clawed with wild desperation at Bolan's sleeves, but the Executioner continued his assault, hammering away with the machine pistol. The seconds of the battle were long and laborious, each savage strike burning more and more of the vital reserves of oxygen in Bolan's bloodstream. The doomsday numbers ticked down to zero, his lungs burning for the sweet freshness of air, but as long as the man was still conscious and struggling, the Executioner didn't dare turn his back on him.

Something bounced against Bolan's back and folded around the two combatants. It was the first of Bolan's underwater victims. With a jerk, Bolan slipped his arm through the sling of the machine pistol. His legs wrapped around the waist of his current wrestling partner and the Executioner twisted, clawing at the dead man. He felt along the chest but found only the hideous fissure he'd hewn from the belly of his first underwater opponent.

A fist arced into Bolan's stomach, but he held his breath, keeping it from bursting from his lips and nostrils. The water resistance that had slowed his own relentless assault saved the Executioner. His fingers clawed for anything on the dead body floating against them.

Finally, his fingertips brushed the wooden stakes of a nunchaku. Initial disappointment soured Bolan's mind, even as his hands grabbed the two lengths of wood, held together by a central chain. Originally used as a rice flail to knock down stalks, peasants had developed a fighting style around this weapon, like they had done with the simple farmer's hand sickle that Bolan initially used. Water resistance, however, would make it useless as a flail.

Even as his brain feverently raced for evaluations of the hand tool, he remembered that one tactic of the nunchaku was to use it to wrap around the blade of a samurai's sword, snagging it and wrenching it from its owner's grasp. Bolan's battle computer mind flashed instantly into action and he wrapped the two-section flail around the neck of his persistant enemy. Crossing the handles, he shifted his grip and twisted hard.

The cultist, with his neck caught between the merciless lengths of wood, thrashed violently, trying to claw himself free. It was too late for him, because the Executioner twisted the nunchaku with all of his might. Bone crunched and bubbles flowed from the dead man's mouth. Neck broken, trachea crushed, the corpse tumbled from between Bolan's legs, black eyes staring glassily at his Executioner.

Bolan had no time to waste. He clutched the pistol grip of

the submachine gun, spearing it ahead of him as he kicked frantically toward the surface. Breaking once more into fresh air, he saw the second cultist on the ledge, jaw slack as the big American surged from the water, submachine gun spitting flame. Bolan's first burst tagged the man in the shoulder, spinning him for an instant. Adjusting his aim, Bolan triggered another two shots, catching the gunman in the forehead, turning his skull into a volcano of brains and blood.

Honey flinched as the last corpse tumbled into the river.

"Swim!" Bolan ordered.

Honey was hanging on to the roots and shook her head, shoulders hunched in fear as well as cold.

"Swim!" Bolan roared.

Honey let go and dropped into the water. She flopped crazily for a moment before dog-paddling clumsily to where Bolan floated.

No one else showed up in the torturous moments it took them to reach the far shore.

Dragging himself to his feet, he did a quick evaluation. Every muscle in his frame ached, and gravity felt as if it were ten times stronger than normal. Honey was on all fours, coughing and gasping, still in six inches of water. Bolan staggered to her side and hooked one hand under her arm.

"Come on," he whispered. "We have to make it to the trees."

Honey limped along. Her weight slowed him, but they still made good time. A bullet barked against a nearby tree trunk and put an extra spring to her ragged step.

The desperate pair disappeared into the woods, leaving the cultists in their wake.

HOGAN MANAGED TO CLAMBER into the helicopter, his shoulders burning with the effort of the frantic climb up the rope ladder. Sinclair slid the cabin door shut.

"What the hell happened?" Sinclair asked.

"We ran into some heavily armed locals," Hogan answered.

"What about the others?" Sinclair asked.

"That bastard Cooper, the FBI agent, he got everyone else."

"I thought you gave him a dud gun," Sinclair said.

Hogan sneered. "That didn't slow him down much. Between him and those psychos chasing me through the woods, they took out everyone from Nickles on down."

Sinclair shook his head. "Damn."

Hogan glared out the window.

"I've got even more bad news," Sinclair told him.

Hogan's eyes rolled to survey his mercenary, his head remaining motionless.

Sinclair opened the laptop on his thighs, swiveling the screen so Hogan could see. A tiny net camera clipped to the top of the screen, taking in the grim scowl on the head mercenary's face.

On the screen, Colin Anthony's handsome face stared out. Black hair, clear blue eyes, a neatly trimmed mustache and a clean, square jaw contrasted against Hogan's blunt, bulletlike head and closely trimmed, crew cut and heavy brow.

"Mr. Anthony—" Hogan began.

"What the hell is going on? You said you'd have my daughter back by now," Anthony cut him off over the link.

"We ran into a problem," Hogan replied.

"What kind of a problem?" Anthony asked, his voice as hard and cold as iron.

"We stumbled onto some kind of terrorist headquarters."

"What?" Anthony asked.

"They attacked both sides," Hogan told him.

"What about Rebecca? And that FBI agent?"

"Rebecca ran off into the woods. We went after her, but I'm the only one left alive."

"And the FBI agent?"

"Him too. It was a total slaughter," Hogan said.

Anthony ran his fingers through his hair, despondance coloring his once stern features. "But Rebecca…"

"She was alive the last I saw her. She was making a beeline for the hills," Hogan said.

"Thank God… What are you doing now?" Anthony asked.

"I'm regrouping. I had some helicopters in reserve, and I'm in one, as you might have guessed," Hogan told him. "We're going to conduct an air search for her."

"Are you sure you'll find her before these other killers?" Anthony asked.

"We've got the best sensor equipment possible on these birds," Hogan answered. "It shouldn't take long to find a single girl in these woods."

"I'm in Tokyo," Anthony said.

Hogan tensed up.

"Is there something wrong?" Anthony asked.

"Just the bullshit I've explained to you," Hogan snapped back. "I can't worry about your safety, not with this mess I'm dealing with."

"You don't have to worry about that. I have my bodyguard with me," Anthony said.

Hogan nodded, hiding his derision at the rich man and his false sense of security. "Just stay put. I'll be in contact with you once we get your girl back."

Hogan waved for Sinclair to kill the connection, and the mercenary did so.

"This is a total fuck-up," Hogan growled. "Now we have that pretty-boy faggot here, trying to check up on us?"

"We are going to look for the girl, though," Sinclair said. "This whole operation is worthless without her."

"Damn straight," Hogan said. "But I lost nineteen men down there."

"We heard three others were alive," Sinclair said. "They must have been captured."

Hogan glanced back down at the forest, his heavy brow furrowing. "Dammit."

"Should we try and get them back?" Sinclair asked.

Hogan didn't tear his gaze from the treetops.

"I said—"

"I heard you!" Hogan snapped. "I don't think those men are going to be too long for this world. Even if we tried to spring them, I don't think we have enough to hit their base. It's too well protected and it didn't look like we could land the helicopters."

"So..." Sinclair began.

"So we find the Anthony girl, we kill Cooper, and just tear ass back to Tokyo," Hogan grumbled. "And we make a stop for the blueprints."

Sinclair nodded numbly.

If his second in command didn't like it, tough, Hogan thought.

Life was full of compromises. And Hogan intended to make sure he lived to see his payoff.

HENDRICKS STAGGERED, shoved by the blunt barrels of submachine guns in the fists of the black-clad cultists. He knew the doorway he was being forced through was probably going to be the last one he'd ever step across. His arm was useless and numbed by the blade that was embedded in his shoulder. The mercenary couldn't fight back if he wanted to.

Dylan and Barlow looked as bad off as he was, covered in cuts and bruises.

"Wait here," one of the guards said. He stepped around Hendricks, keeping a wary eye on the mercenary as he walked up a set of wooden stairs. A red satin banner, with an embroidered black serpent hung over the staircase.

A Japanese man in black robes, a red version of the banner serpent adorning one side of his body, appeared at the top of the steps. He had a black goatee, and while he wasn't a big man, he had an aura of authority. Black eyes fixed on Hendricks, and the mercenary, froze in fear.

"You are tresspassers upon the lands of I, Master Zakoji," he said.

Zakoji seemed to glide down the steps, his feet hidden by the length of his robes. But it was close enough to the ghost-like hovering of something not quite alive, not quite natural, that it made Hendricks tremble.

Zakoji closed in on the trio and lifted one long finger. The fingernail extended out like a talon, and its sharp tip scratched along Hendricks's chin. The mercenary recoiled from the scrape. He felt like the hand of death itself had brushed his soul.

"You did not answer me, foreign dogs," Zakoji snarled.

"We have rights!" Barlow spoke up. Dylan stepped away from him. Barlow glanced at his fellow prisoner, wondering why he wasn't standing up with him.

"Take him," Zakoji growled.

Two of Zakoji's minions rushed forward and gripped Barlow tightly. The mercenary struggled, squirming against their strong grasp. Hendricks and Dylan remained silent, knowing that any form of defiance would be the kiss of death. Though the two were fighting men, they knew full well that when you were a prisoner, compliance was the surest tactic for survival. Barlow had just committed the gravest error of his soon to be very short life.

"Where...where are you taking him?" Dylan asked, the fear in his voice softening his question, lowering his tone to that of deference to the ominous black-robed Zakoji.

"To put on a demonstration for you," Zakoji said coldly.

Hendricks's throat dried, and when he tried to swallow, it was almost unbearable. Whatever was about to happen, he knew it would haunt his nightmares for as long as he lived.

Provided he survived to sleep peacefully again.

**11**

Honey was limping severely. Bolan was holding her up, half carrying her, and they weren't making quick progress. The Executioner's body was stiffening from the cold, and he knew that Honey was suffering even more. He was used to being out in the cold and exposed to the chill air.

Honey stared at the ground ahead of her, hobbling along, tucked tight into Bolan's armpit. Her lips trembled, and her jaw was clenched to keep her teeth from biting her tongue as they chattered. Her fists drew her clothes tight across her shoulders, and she held the soaking mess so hard, her knuckles were white.

"Just a little farther," Bolan told her.

Honey didn't look up. The young woman was unresponsive, so Bolan stopped. Honey's feet kept moving, and she would have pulled away from him had he not firmly locked his arm across her shoulders. He held her tight and after a few more abortive steps to pull forward, she stopped and just shook in his embrace.

"Honey…"

She didn't look up at his words. Bolan gave her cheek a sharp slap. That made her blink, and her grip released on the shoulder of her blouse, rising to the stinging flesh.

"Honey…snap out of it," Bolan said.

He realized she was hypothermic, and she was already going into shock. The soldier looked around desperately. In the middle of these woods, he wouldn't be able to light a fire. It would draw the attention of far too many enemies.

"Sorry," Honey slurred. Her eyes were still unfocused, but she was moving a little more now. "Cold," was all she managed to say.

"I know," Bolan told her. They were almost to where he'd buried the vests, the spare pistols and martial-arts weapons. He bent and scooped her up, carrying her in his sore, protesting arms.

Bolan lost his balance more than once, but he only dropped to his knees, his back racked with pain as he fought to keep Honey from falling. Struggling back to his feet after his last stumble, he lurched towards the tree where he'd half buried the leftovers from the battle with the cultists. Four corpses lay near the roots of a great tree, and one thick tendril over was his cache.

Bolan set Honey down and began stripping the dead men of their clothing. Blood had crusted on the collars and down the backs, but it was no longer wet.

"Honey, get undressed," Bolan told her.

Honey rested against the trunk of the tree, staring at nothing. She blankly rubbed her hands up and down her biceps through her soaking sleeves. Bolan turned back and began pulling her out of her blouse. Honey shrugged away from him.

"Honey, you're going to only get worse if you don't get out of your wet clothes," Bolan said. He grabbed her again, and she pushed him away.

"All right," she murmured. She sounded drunk, but it meant her brain was still working, despite the numbing effects of the cold.

"Come on," Bolan said. "I'll help."

Honey nodded and grabbed the hem of her blouse and tore it open. It slid off her arms. Her black tank top stuck to her freckled chest.

"That too," Bolan told her, almost apologetically.

Honey nodded and hooked the bottom, peeling it from her wet skin. Underneath, she wore a black lace bra and a couple chains. One of the chains was an Egyptian Ankh, and the other was a Celtic Knot wrought in pewter. Honey looked down and then seemed to have to drag her eyes back to look at Bolan.

"Bra too?" she asked.

Bolan weighed his options, then handed her the black tunic and T-shirt of one of the dead men. "No, that will dry quickly," he said.

Bolan laid the clothes in her. He could see that Honey didn't spend much effort eating. Her body was almost painfully slender. Bolan took a T-shirt and used it as an improvised towel, wiping off her wet skin.

Honey looked at him. "Thanks."

"Get the T-shirt and tunic on."

Honey slipped the T-shirt over her head. "At least these guys like black too," she said and smiled.

Bolan shook his head. "Fashionable commandos are a common breed."

Honey's shoulders shook for a moment as she tugged the T-shirt into place. It was a little baggy on her, but at least it wasn't constricting her. Bolan waited for her to shrug into the tunic and pull it tight around her.

"That better?" Bolan asked.

Honey nodded, still looking small and tired. Bolan knew how she felt. He just wished that the dead enemies he encountered had bigger builds. He mopped off his chest and arms with one of the dead men's shirts, then experimentally shrugged into the biggest tunics he could find. The sleeves were stretched taut across his biceps and shoulders. It hung open on his chest, and Bolan flexed.

Seams ripped and popped, and it felt a little looser now.

What was more, he felt a little warmer. Not much, but it was some protection. His bare chest, however, was exposed. Vents had been ripped in the backs of the arms and the tops of the shoulders, letting in the cool breeze.

Bolan twisted his waist, checking his range of motion. More seams tore under the stretching, and the Executioner wondered how long the tunic would last. He glanced at Honey, who had slipped out the rest of her wet clothes and her remaining shoe.

"I need pants," Honey murmured. Exhaustion was evident in her voice. Bolan peeled a pair off one of the corpses. He grabbed the boots off a dead man's feet and helped wrestle her into them.

"Yeah," Honey said. "Footwear is good."

Bolan nodded, then mopped the girl's head with the T-shirt. "Feeling warmer?"

"A little," Honey answered. Bolan sat next to her, slipping his arm around her.

"Just sharing body heat," Bolan told her.

Honey rested her head against his shoulder. "I figured."

Bolan took a deep breath and was thankful for the bulk of the tree sheltering them. He reached down to one of the pistols he collected, a SIG-Sauer P-228. He checked its load, and it had a full 13-round magazine, one up the spout. He lowered the hammer with the decocker and tucked it between his legs. He also made sure that the katana was propped up next to his leg.

Having a quiet weapon would mean the difference between safety and discovery.

The Executioner worked himself tighter against Honey, and let her fall asleep against his side.

She needed the rest, and so did he.

BARLOW STARTED TO SWEAT when he realized that the two men flanking him were wearing rubberized Nuclear-Biological-Chemical suits, their thick-gloved hands gripping his forearms with cruel strength. He pulled and tugged as they pushed him toward an air lock. He glanced back and knew that Hendricks and Dylan were still under the guns of Lord Zakoji.

"Please, I'm sorry," Barlow begged. He tried to twist free, but the Japanese men had incredible strength. A third man raced to the air lock and punched in a sequence on the keypad.

The door hissed open, revealing a darkened chamber. Barlow was pushed through the doorway, and he crashed against the far door. He turned to try to break free, but the stock of a rifle swung and struck him in the stomach, dropping him to his knees. The mercenary looked up helplessly as he watched the outer door hiss closed.

The door behind him opened slightly, and Barlow looked over his shoulder. The room was empty, sterile white. He was terrified, but he stepped into the room.

He saw three people. Their faces were covered in sores, black reddened blotches. Froth covered their lips, and their clothes were in torn and bloody tatters. All of them were Japanese, two men and one woman.

The whites of their eyes had turned as red as blood.

It was like a scene out of a horror movie. Jerking spasmodically, they looked around, blinking at the brilliant whiteness of the room. Under the tatters of their clothes their skin was raw from scratching on their arms and chests. What wasn't clawed was brilliant red with blood, or darkened to deep purple with more of the hideous blotches.

One of the two men gave a mighty jerk and collapsed to the floor where he lay trembling, spitting up more foam from his lips.

The other man and woman glared at Barlow.

"Stay away," the mercenary whispered. He stepped back toward the air lock.

The woman reached out, her mouth opening and closing, gasping for air. Her fingernails were broken and shattered, crusted with dried blood. She grabbed his arm, and Barlow punched her hard in the jaw.

"I said get away!"

The woman's head recoiled, and her chewed lips drew back in a craggy toothed sneer. The other man lunged, shoving the woman aside.

Barlow brought up his knee, throwing the man back over the jerking, spastic form on the floor. He fell with a dull thud and struggled to get up. Foam escaped from his lips. The woman lurched at him, hissing wildly.

Whether it was an attack, or her simply grasping at him for help, Barlow neither knew nor cared. He backhanded the sick woman across the face and threw her to the ground. His skin started to tingle. A burning sensation ran up and down his forearm where she'd grabbed him, and Barlow tore his sleeve free, feeling as if it were on fire.

Red splotches were forming on his arm, and in the middle of each, he saw the almost microscopic forms of fleas, digging into his flesh to suck his blood. He slapped at the skin, trying to beat them away. His fingers clawed at the parasites as they continued to feed. He raked harder, drawing his own blood.

He understood why the people looked like zombies with

tattered flesh. They were trying to get rid of the hideous burning of the flea bites, and the infection that the damnable insects would inflict.

An uncontrollable tremor ran through Barlow's body. If he didn't know any better, he'd have sworn he was suffering from the bubonic plague, but he knew it took four to seven days for symptoms of the plague to take effect.

Barlow clenched his jaws tightly and looked around. He was burning with fever, and his salivary glands were releasing wildly. He was foaming at the mouth, as if he were rabid.

He thought about the fleas.

It seemed that somehow, the parasites had piggybacked two deadly diseases in one. And he was succumbing to both of them far faster than he would have any normal case.

"Let me out of—"

The first jolt of pain sizzled through him. His brain felt as if it were burning, assaulted by the twin forces of fever and rabies. He collapsed to his knees, instinct taking over.

"No," Barlow murmured. He clawed at the wall, digging at the white purity, leaving streaks of crimson. "Please!"

He looked at the corner of the room, where a dome of white plastic was visible. The dazzled vestiges of his consciousness recognized it as a hidden camera. He lurched toward it, hands banging at the curvature of the half sphere. Barlow collapsed, brushing the bottom of it with a wild swing.

He curled up in agony.

HENDRICKS WATCHED as his friend and partner was reduced to a quivering pile in the space of twenty minutes. His mouth was dry, and he glanced toward Zakoji, who simply smiled.

"What...what was that?"

"I managed to crossbreed fleas," Zakoji said.

"Fleas?" Hendricks asked. Dylan was silent, his eyes wide with horror.

"Yes. The perfect little blood-sucking, contagion-spreading monsters that nearly annihilated Europe centuries ago," Zakoji said.

"But…" Hendricks began. "The plague?"

"An upgraded form of the plague," Zakoji replied. "It's taken a few years, but I've finally managed to make a plague bacterium which is host to another virus."

"A virus?" Hendricks asked.

"Rabies," Zakoji said. "We had a few Australian bats with their version of the virus, and isolated it. After that, it simply took a little work to integrate it with a bacterium cell."

Hendricks looked aghast.

"The rabies virus replicates through infecting cells. Bacteria, being plant-based, not animal-based, weren't the ideal home for the virus, not at first. However, bacterial gestation is quite rapid. You can have five generations of bacteria in the space of a day with the right species," Zakoji explained. He smirked at Hendricks. "Don't you love when nature provides the perfect weapons?"

Hendricks was slack jawed. "But…but he started suffering almost immediately."

"A side effect of piggybacking the two organisms. Actually, the hypermetabolizing version of the bacteria has been slowly dying out, while the version that has a more normal time frame of development is surviving long enough to breed true and transmit. The people who suffer from it still begin suffering in three days, not the usual four to seven days."

"But…"

"Just a test subject. The victims go mad with pain after exposure. The fleas also congregate around dead bodies. We've been digging them up from the Yakuza landfill, and they've been breeding in the carcasses, feeding on dead flesh as well as fresh blood," Zakoji explained. "It's very complicated, but my biologists assure me that these little bugs are going to be able to survive in Tokyo's alleys."

Hendricks paled.

"Traditionally, Asia has managed to keep the plague quarantined to the Chinese mainland. It's a tough effort, but once we start importing them to downtown Tokyo…"

Hendricks looked at Zakoji. "But…what are you going to do with us?"

Zakoji looked him over. "Further testing is required. I just thought I'd give you a glimpse of your future."

Hendricks looked back to the video screen, then turned and lunged at Zakoji, hands extended forward like talons. The Japanese man sidestepped the assault, raising an arm as hard as ironwood.

Hendricks took the forearm across his throat, and his head snapped back. He skidded to the floor in a mad tumble. Other guards rose to restrain the mercenary, but Zakoji waved them away.

"You wish to have the quick way out?" Zakoji asked. "Good. I need some exercise."

Hendricks rose, coughing from the savage clothesline to his throat. He was still gasping for breath when Zakoji stepped in, hooking his fingers into the mercenary's collarbone. With a powerful spin, he hurled the larger American across the floor.

Hendricks's tumble stopped at the feet of a sentry, and the mercenary reached up. The cultist wound up to backhand the prisoner, but Zakoji cut him off with a sharp command in Japanese. The guard presented a sword to Hendricks.

The mercenary looked at the blade's handle, then back at the robed cult leader.

"Take it," Zakoji said.

From the folds of his black, serpent-embroidered robes, Zakoji drew his own gleaming length of steel. The cult leader's lips curled in a mocking smirk as both of his hands closed on the silk-cord wrapped pommel of his blade.

Hendricks clutched the offered sword and spun to face the Japanese man. He knew next to nothing about the use of a sword, but he counted on his greater size and longer reach. If I'm going to die, he thought, it will be as a lion, not a cowering monkey. He took three quick strides across the room and swung the sword like a baseball bat.

Zakoji easily deflected the clumsy stroke with a mere flip of his own blade. Steel sung on steel, and Hendricks was thrown off balance by the force of his own swing. Zakoji stepped in and raked the point of his blade, almost playfully, across Hendricks's belly, opening his black uniform shirt. The tender skin was scratched, a light trickle of blood welling up.

It was a minor wound. Hendricks looked down at it, his entire body flushed with sweat as he struggled to grip his sword tighter. Zakoji cooly pointed the tip of his sword toward the floor. Then slowly, casually, he brought both arms up.

At least it looked casual. Hendricks could see the veins in Zakoji's powerful forearms standing out as he raised the sword above his head, sleeves falling away to display rockhard muscles. Zakoji's cocky smile disappeared behind a mask of stone-hard concentration.

Hendricks had seen enough samurai movies to know that his opponent was preparing for a lethal stroke. He didn't want to give the man a chance and lunged forward, swinging his sword again.

In a flicker of movement, Zakoji had the sword lowered,

point toward the floor. Hendricks swung his shoulders hard, but he completely missed the Japanese man. It took a moment for the pain to register. Hendricks screamed as he saw the sword he once held, clattered on the far side of the room, and both of his arms bleeding profusely. His legs gave out under him and he threw a curse at the cult leader.

Zakoji took a half step and brought up his own silk-handled sword. Hendricks felt something sting his chin. He opened his mouth to speak, but his lips and tongue suddenly gushed forth a torrent of blood. Hendricks wanted to reach up to hold his face, now erupting with gore from where Zakoji's final slash had split it open, but his brain was already shutting down.

Zakoji shook his head, then drew the sword back swiftly in a horizontal arc.

Darkness descended on Hendricks and he never felt the final blow.

ZAKOJI LEANED DOWN and wiped Hendricks's blood from his blade edge, then glared at Dylan.

"You too wish mercy?" Zakoji asked.

Dylan's struggles had stopped.

"Just say the word, and I'll let you pick up your friend's sword," the cult leader told him.

Dylan stared at his friend's lifeless form.

"Send him to his friend in the testing room," Zakoji said.

Dylan was dragged away.

Zakoji resheathed his blade.

Toshiee stepped up. "Lord and master! We've got a report on the two captives we lost."

Zakoji tilted his head, waiting for the young man to speak.

Toshiee took the cue and continued. "They left the river, and we followed them on the seismic sensor until they entered the blind spot where our motion detector shorted out earlier today."

"And where we lost the four-man patrol," Zakoji said. "He must have stored extra weapons and gear there."

"I am going to lead a team to that sector," Toshiee stated.

"And the other men? The Yakuza?" Zakoji asked.

"There are five of them," Toshiee noted. "And they are heading to the same location."

"Really?" Zakoji asked. "You think they're trying to connect with the others?"

"Yes," Toshiee answered. "It only makes sense. They made an effort to rescue the Americans. Perhaps they feel there is strength in numbers."

"Particularly the man. He claimed the lives of five men in his escape, even though he started out unarmed and bound at the wrists," Zakoji noted. "So skilled a warrior could mean the difference between life and death when facing a superior enemy."

Toshiee nodded. "We will be merciless and certain with him, unless you wish us to take him alive."

Zakoji shook his head. "No. Kill him and the girl and the gangsters. I wish to cleanse my valley."

Toshiee bowed his head to his leader.

"But keep an eye out for the helicopters. I don't want to lose any more of my men, and those flying gunships can do us irreperable harm," Zakoji said. "Rikyu, the Syrians gave us some lovely antiaircraft missiles."

"I have already had the guard posts issued with them," Rikyu answered.

"Good," Zakoji said.

A good fighting force was hard to find, but his men were organized.

And even if this mysterious American warrior were the

Shogun's executioner reincarnated, he was cursed to die in this valley by his predecessor.

The American was just a man, and he would die as easily as any other.

**12**

The rustle of leaves in the distance snapped Bolan's eyes awake. Though he was still tired, he woke from his combat nap with all his senses in order. He brought up the SIG-Sauer P-228 with one hand, the handle of the sword in his other. Bolan rose to a crouch, angling the blade of the katana across his body to guard himself.

"Cooper!" a voice whispered. "Cooper! Don't shoot!"

Bolan didn't recognize the voice, but he did pick up the Japanese accent in the English-speaking voice. Honey stirred at his side, her big blue eyes blinking gummily.

Bolan remained quiet, but he still had his finger on the trigger. Twelve pounds of pressure, and he'd send a 9 mm slug into the first hostile form.

"Machida?" Honey murmured.

"Cooper! I want to talk. I'm unarmed."

Bolan glared at Honey in hopes of keeping her silent. Instead, she scrambled to a crouch and bobbed her head to get a look at the approaching Yakuza man. Bolan rested his wrist on her shoulder to calm her down.

Machida stepped into view, hands above his head. He was wearing body armor over a muddy, rumpled suit, and his short black hair was flyaway, stiffened by sweat after becoming windblown. He was unarmed, though he had holsters and spare magazine pouches stripped from dead cultists.

"Agent Cooper, I want to ask you for help," Machida said.

"Stay right there," Bolan told him. He crouched behind the snarled, thick tendril of a root, keeping the P-228's front sight on Machida.

"I'd like to stand here all day, Cooper, but we have to hurry," Machida said.

Bolan glanced around. He couldn't pick up the sounds of others trying to flank him, though he knew that Machida wasn't alone.

"Where are your friends?" Bolan asked.

"If you're talking about Hogan, I left him behind," Machida answered.

"And that should make me trust you?" Bolan asked.

"I'm not asking you for blind faith, Agent Cooper. But we're in a situation where people are trying to kill us. You've proved to be the most capable fighter I've ever seen," Machida said. "I need help, and that means I need you on my side."

"In case you forgot, I'm FBI, and you're Yakuza."

Machida shrugged. "Do you think those cultists really care?"

Bolan eased his finger off the trigger. "And what about Hogan?"

"I'd hoped that he'd be killed when we caused the diversion that enabled your escape," Machida responded. "I doubt it, though, because I heard helicopters."

"He called in backup," Bolan said.

"We both did, but I don't have faith in my fellow street soldiers to engage in a battle against an army of terrorists in a forest. Not when they have better weapons than we do," Machida said. "You, however, started unarmed but slaughtered several heavily armed and armored mercenaries and my own men."

"And how do I know you won't go for some payback for those dead men?" Bolan asked. His finger curled around the trigger of his pistol again.

"Maybe somewhere down the line, after this is over. But right now, my survival hinges on my being with the right person. You are that person," Machida told him.

"Very flattering," Bolan answered. "What's in it for me?"

"You have a group of men under your command now. Allies. Extra guns. You won't be fighting alone," Machida replied.

"And your boys will work with me, after the damage I've done to them?" Bolan asked.

"They're interested in living."

Bolan kept his eyes peeled, scanning the forest. "Tell them to come forward."

Machida turned and rattled off a quick command in Japanese. Shapes shifted in the trees behind him, and then stepped forward. The men had their guns lowered, but they were still armed. Bolan redirected his attention toward them.

"Honey, please, tell Agent Cooper that I meant you no harm," Machida said.

Honey looked to Cooper, then back to the Yakuza man. "He really seemed disgusted with the guys he was working with," she said.

Bolan looked at her from the corner of his eye. "That doesn't mean that he isn't going to try to kill me and take you captive again at the first opportunity."

Honey looked down. "But he's right about the fact that we can't stop Zakoji alone."

Bolan bristled, his every instinct telling him that he was making a deal with the devil. No matter what Honey felt about the Yakuza headman, he was still part of an organization that had built itself on the backs of extortion, murder, drug dealing, smuggling and sexual slavery.

Destroying Machida's Yakuza clan was Bolan's first priority, the very reason he'd ended up in this viper's pit. And trading one devil for another...

He remembered an old piece of wisdom that had carried him through several campaigns. Pitting one enemy against another had granted him the ability to outnumber forces that swamped him hundreds to one. Bolan had played both angles before. He'd even teamed with devils, but always watched his back. More often than not, in his fragile, tenuous alliances, he had to react instantly to a last-minute betrayal. Those had been close calls, and sometimes they'd ended in tragedy.

Bolan looked at Honey. She was brash, and an unusually tough-hearted young girl. For her to identify with Machida, to seem almost happy to see him alive, gave Bolan a moment's pause before he reevaluated the man.

"I know we're outnumbered," Bolan told her. "But..."

"You're just one man. Sure, you've chewed through almost everyone we've run into, but look at you," Honey snapped.

Bolan knew she was right. He was beaten, battered and exhausted.

"Cooper, I know that this cult has some means of detecting movement. They've certainly been monitoring our movements, and the fact that we're standing here means we've made ourselves a target," Machida said.

"I took out a seismic sensor, not far from here," Bolan said. "I'm not sure the exact diameter of their blind spot, but it's something."

Machida tilted his head. "You're trusting me with that?"

"You said it yourself. We're up against some long odds," Bolan told him. He stood up, still gripping the pistol and the katana. "I know it's in your interests to keep the girl alive too."

Machida nodded and took a step forward.

Bolan lifted the sword tip and pointed it at Machida. "But

I also know you'd like nothing more than to have me out of your way. I won't let you have the blueprints you came for. And I won't let the girl go without a fight."

Machida nodded. "I did not doubt that. And undoubtedly, you'd pick me as the first to die."

Bolan shook his head. "I'd take out the most direct threat first. But don't take it personally. I'd get to you eventually."

Machida managed a weak smile. "Then we have a temporary alliance?"

"Yes," Bolan answered.

The other Yakuza men jogged forward, picking up their pace. One handed some guns off to Machida, while another walked toward Bolan and Honey, holding out a machine pistol as a peace offering.

"You'll need more firepower than just a pistol," Machida told him. "Especially if you're going to help protect Honey."

Bolan took the gun and a couple spare magazines. "These are from the cultists," he said.

Machida nodded. "Thank Hogan. He suggested we upgrade from hunting rifles and pistols to something heavier."

Honey bent and picked up one of the other two SIG-Sauer pistols that Bolan had collected, and stuffed it into her waistband. She gave Bolan a nervous glance.

"It's safe," Bolan told her.

Honey gave a curt nod. She looked back to Machida, and Bolan was pleased to see that she'd made a defiant show of arming herself. She wasn't going to let herself be taken either.

Bolan was starting to feel better about the situation.

THE HELICOPTER HOVERED over the clearing where the vehicles were congregated. Hogan let Sinclair go down for the blueprints while he stayed in the chopper.

Hogan would have gone himself, he was the kind of man who preferred to do as much as possible on his own, but he was exhausted, battered, bruised. His hand didn't feel right, ever since Cooper took a shot at him and ripped the machine gun out of his grip. Still, he leaned out the door, looking down at Sinclair as he tossed the van.

"It's not here!" Sinclair shouted over the mike.

Hogan leaned out further. He frowned.

"Someone cleaned out the vans. They did a thorough job yanking out all the panels. The locks were shot off," Sinclair explained.

Hogan banged his fist against the helicopter's door frame. "Dammit."

He slumped back into his seat, cursing himself. The cultists had jumped them, and he'd assumed that keeping the blueprints locked tightly away would have granted him some breathing space to turn around and head back to recover them. He'd underestimated his enemies, and despite having the plans secreted away, he hadn't counted on their desire to get everything. That meant, of course, the cultists had control of spare radios, grenades, rocket launchers, and the extra weapons and ammo that had been stashed in the van.

Hogan grumbled.

They were good. Too damn good.

"We're going to have to break into their headquarters and take back our blueprints," Hogan said.

"A full, coordinated assault. We only have the crews of the helicopters," Sinclair said. "That and a couple of extra soldiers."

Hogan frowned. "If we can soften them up enough, we should stand a chance. The helicopters can rain enough mayhem on them to get us past their defenses and into their base."

Sinclair frowned. "Too risky. What if they shoot down our

birds? They have our rockets, and given their preparations, they might have something for aircraft too."

Hogan grimaced. Sinclair was right. He'd lost too damn many men by underestimating his enemies. The cultists and Cooper had torn his mercenaries apart as if they were paper targets.

"All right. A frontal assault would be suicide. Besides, I don't want to waste any more fuel than I have to," Hogan said. "Set this bird down."

The other helicopters had found a clearing by the river and were idling.

"Power down the other birds," he ordered over the headset.

"Roger that," the other pilots answered.

Hogan's helicopter landed a little way from the cars and Sinclair jogged up.

"I'm thinking a stealth penetration. Once we locate the blueprints, we can call in air support," Sinclair said. "After we take out the rocket crews."

"That'll mean waiting for it to get a little darker. A crawl like that through their base will take time, and plenty of darkness," Hogan surmised.

"It's not a perfect plan, and they'll be on alert for us," Sinclair replied.

"I'm not losing those blueprints to a bunch of psychos," Hogan said.

"You're underestimating them," Sinclair said.

"Oh, I respect them. I'm just not willing to give up that easily."

"And the girl?" Sinclair asked.

"We'll call off the aerial patrols I planned for tonight. It'll make our birds too easy a target for heat seekers," Hogan said. He frowned. "Besides, knowing Cooper, he'd be getting close to the locals."

"Why? He was here to rescue the girl," Sinclair said.

"He *said* he was here to rescue the girl. A guy like that, if something pops up on his radar, he focuses on it like a laser. Cooper sees this bunch of wackos as a serious threat, and he's not going to sit on the sidelines and let someone else take care of business for him," Hogan stated.

Sinclair tilted his head. "Just one man?"

"Look at the damage he's done to our group already," Hogan responded.

"Color me corrected," Sinclair answered. "So you think he'll be around the enemy base too?"

"To take out the bad guys, to do his absolute worst to make their lives a living hell. He'll park the girl somewhere safe, but close enough that he can retrieve her."

"Sounds like a risk."

Hogan nodded. "A big risk, but this guy knows how to take risks and keep on going. He leads a charmed life, but mainly because he's too smart, too skilled, and too lucky to get taken down by a single accident."

Hogan flexed his injured hand.

Yeah, Cooper was still a threat, he thought, and if luck was on his side, the big bastard was going to be making his penetration, around the time they were.

If they ran across each other, then Hogan was going to make sure that only he was left standing.

TOSHIEE GRIPPED his submachine gun, leading his group of fellow Burakku Uwibami clansmen through the forest. According to the main base, none of the people they were tracking had moved from the blind spot where their network of seismic sensors had lost one of its motion detecting eyes. Toshiee was tense.

Not only were they going after two Americans, who had

managed to break out of captivity with the aid of a diversion and by killing no less than five of their own number while poorly armed, there were five unknown figures who were the final survivors of the small army that had invaded their territory. According to reports from their fellow Black Serpents who had taken apart the vehicles owned by the intruders, it was a mixture of local Yakuza, and well-armed and well-equipped mercenaries. If they were going to run up against the American and the mercenaries, Toshiee knew he and his fellow Black Serpents would be in for a fight.

On his hip was a *wakazashi* short sword, a concession toward the Burakku Uwibami's vow to return to the ways of feudal Japan. But Toshiee would only use that if he ran out of ammunition for the deadly little Uzi submachine gun in his hands. It was ironic that the Lord Master Zakoji chose to use the tools of the outsiders, Israeli submachine guns, Syrian biological weaponry, American seismic detectors and mobile communications equipment, to roust the enemy. But then, desperate measures were needed against such a wall of modern force as the European invaders who were squeezing the heritage from Japan.

Toshiee shook himself from his meditations, keeping his eyes and ears peeled for traces of the intruders.

Toshiee glanced back to his men. There were six of them, and they were armed to the teeth as he was, with a mixture of ancient and modern weaponry. Bullets and blades, buckshot and spears, all for the purpose of bringing down their enemies.

Movement ahead caught his eye. Toshiee waved for his men to stop and crouched, his eyes narrowing as he tried to make out details in the distance.

The Black Serpents remained quiet and stealthy, spreading out slowly, their feet treading softly, avoiding the rustle of ground clutter and snapping twigs. When the group formed a half circle, all keeping their eyes on the movement ahead, they stopped and waited for Toshiee's word to advance.

The young leader nodded and crawled forward, keeping the muzzle of his Uzi pointed at the mysterious motion through the tree trunks. He paused when he cleared one bush, seeing it was something tied to a branch, flapping in the breeze. It was a gauzy black shirt, like the one the girl had worn when she was captured. Confusion raced across Toshiee's features as he looked at the fluttering garment.

Advancing further, Toshiee closed the distance between himself and the makeshift flag, curiosity drawing him closer and closer into range.

Something rustled above him, and the Black Serpent looked up in time to see the Executioner sail down from a branch, smashing him in the chest with both feet. Toshiee was slammed onto his back. His ribs were shattered by the force of Bolan's landing. He could barely move as the big American fanned short bursts of autofire at his fellow Black Serpents. The cultists cried out as from hidden parts of the forest, muzzle-flashes flared and spit flame and lead at the group.

Toshiee forced himself back into motion. His submachine gun had been cast aside in the impact, and he didn't know where it was, but he still had his sword on his hip. Grabbing the handle, he pulled the short blade from its sheath, steel glimmering in the dying evening light.

"Cooper!" Machida called from one side.

The Executioner leaped into the air as Toshiee's sword almost sliced him off at the calves. Landing on the other side of the swing, Bolan stomped at the Black Serpent's arm, but missed as the young cultist rolled out of the way.

Bolan swung his submachine gun toward the young Japanese man. The sword flicked up again and sang off the barrel of the weapon, Bolan's burst chewing the ground three feet to the right of the downed cultist.

With obvious effort, Toshiee lurched to a crouch and swung the sword again. Bolan caught the next blade stroke on the barrel of his assault weapon. Both men were driven backward by the force of their colliding steel, Bolan's Uzi slipping from his grasp. Toshiee tightened his grasp on his sword and took a quick step forward, slicing the air where the Executioner's chest had been only moments before.

Bolan was too swift, tumbling away from the deadly slash. Rather than grope for one of his spare pistols, he instead grabbed the handle of his own katana and brought it up to meet Toshiee's next assault. Again metal rang against metal, but this time Bolan's grip on the hilt was surer, and he retained his weapon. Toshiee backed up, keeping the blade in front of him in a defensive posture.

Bolan knew that while he had the longer of the swords, and his own arms were longer than his opponent's, giving him almost a foot and a half advantage in reach, the Black Serpent had trained with the sword more intensively. Although the Executioner had engaged in deadly duels with sword-wielding opponents in the past, he had won through determination and resourcefulness, as well as recently acquired skill.

Still, he lunged, extending the point of his katana like a fencer, aiming for Toshiee's belly. Instead of burying itself in viscera, the glimmering ribbon of metal flickered through empty air, screeching as the cultist's sword met his side on. With the impact Bolan stumbled, half thrown off balance.

The Executioner realized that he couldn't count on his physical condition being better than the Black Serpent's. Though blood was trickling from the Japanese man's mouth, Bolan himself was exhausted, his muscles still sore from the savage, desperate battles against far too many enemies. With a flick of his wrist, he barely managed to deflect Toshiee's counterstrike, stepping out of the path of the cutting edge of the enemy steel.

Pivoting, Bolan brought down his sword, slicing through Toshiee's shoulder in a wild gamble to take out his foe. Bolan felt his own confiscated Kevlar vest part, ripped by the curved point of the enemy blade. Something warm trickled down his side, and Bolan knew that Toshiee had managed to draw first blood.

Gripping the *wakazashi* with one hand, the young Black Serpent's other arm hung limply. The fresh wound bled profusely, and Toshiee's eyes had glazed over. He was halfway to going into shock, but when Bolan feinted at him with his longer sword, the Japanese cultist still managed to block the false stroke, and bring the short blade around to knock away his second, true attack.

Gunfire split the air again, and Toshiee cringed as he took a shot in his own body armor. He half turned, looking at Honey Anthony, holding a pistol. The Black Serpent took a step toward her, and Bolan took the opening.

His katana sliced through nylon and Kevlar and sunk into Toshiee's chest. Bone and flesh separated with the force of Bolan's blade stroke, and when he brought the cutting edge out of the cultist's back, a spray of blood followed. Toshiee shuddered violently with the lethal slash, vomiting bright crimson as the Executioner had sliced completely through one lung, his aorta, and half of his other lung.

Cut nearly in two, the Black Serpent tumbled lifelessly to the ground in a puddle of bloody mud.

Bolan took a deep breath, then tore open his vest to look at his own injury. It was a scratch, maybe a half-inch in depth. Any deeper, and Bolan would be in serious trouble.

Machida came up to him, tearing a strip from the hem of his shirt. "You'll need a bandage."

He accepted the cloth and Machida's tie. "Is everyone else accounted for?" Bolan asked.

The Yakuza man nodded. "We've doubled our firepower as well. Plenty of fresh ammunition. There was also a giant among the gunmen."

Bolan raised an eyebrow.

"Well, he was over six feet," Machida said.

The Executioner nodded.

"His uniform tunic is mostly intact, as is his body armor. That should be enough for you to be more comfortable."

"Worried about me getting too cold?" Bolan asked.

"I want you in top fighting condition. That means you have to be warmly dressed and well armed. I'm sorry you don't have time to rest, but we can't have everything," Machida replied.

"If we did, we'd have a small army of trained soldiers, complete with air support," Bolan answered.

"Well, we have called in backup, but we're too far from the cliff where we had our ill-fated meeting," Machida said. "They're not forest trackers."

Bolan glanced up in the darkness, remembering his bearings and finding the cliff. They were two miles from it, and in the dark, they'd be followed easily by the Black Serpents.

There was also Hogan and his helicopters to worry about.

"Your plan of getting to their headquarters and stopping Zakoji is the only one we have," Machida said. "Stealth and audacity are our best tools."

Bolan nodded. "I've known that for years."

"Darkness has finally fallen," Machida said. "Let's see who the shadows favor more, us or the Black Serpents."

Bolan finished fastening the pad made from Machida's

torn shirt to his side with the tie. It wouldn't move too much, and he accepted the blood-spattered shirt of the dead Japanese cultist who was nearly his size. It was still tight across his broad shoulders, but his arms and waist had freedom of motion. The Kevlar body armor was also snug, but that would help to keep the pressure on Bolan's improvised bandage.

"The shadows, luck, the gods of war, I prefer to make my own fortune," Bolan said.

Machida nodded. "Then siding with a warrior who leaves nothing to chance was my wisest of tactics today."

In the fading light, Bolan could barely see the Yakuza man's smile. He fought the urge to like this man. They were enemies, only at truce because they faced a far worse mutual threat.

Respect for the enemy was something that the Executioner always had. It kept him alive, realizing their worth, their skills, their determination. Admiration, however, was something that he could hardly afford, when sooner or later, their own swords were going to cross.

And when that happened, Bolan knew only one man would walk away.

**13**

Botan Okudaira was not a man to let lackeys do too much of his work. He'd trusted Hideaki Machida with the task of delivering the kidnapped Rebecca Anthony to her father's mercenaries in exchange for a ransom of money and blueprints. But, when they received the phone call from Unno requesting assistance, Okudaira knew that he couldn't let someone else take the risks for him, not anymore.

Something had obviously gone horribly wrong. Okudaira had sent twenty of his finest men under Machida. The Yakuza bossman had his own elite group of bodyguards, each of them highly trained specialists in not only protection, but in all manner of street warfare. Obviously, if there was a problem, it had to have been that Anthony's mercenaries were far better armed and trained.

Okudaira dreaded coming upon the meeting scene, knowing he would find a massacre.

Instead, one of his men came back to him, slipping his night-vision goggles up onto his forehead. Kenji was almost six feet tall and powerfully built. He was the kind of hardman that Okudaira wanted in one of his elite enforcers.

"Sir, there is a helicopter armed with a machine gun at the clearing. The vehicles have all been wrecked, and there are some bodies on the ground," the bodyguard said.

"Our men?"

"I recognized some of our own, but there were only a few. There were also the mercenaries, but again, only a handful of dead," Kenji answered.

Okudaira furrowed his brow. "They were driven away?"

Kenji shrugged, uncertain of the situation. "Both sets of vehicles, our own and the mercenaries' were wrecked. Someone seems to have disabled them, then searched them thoroughly."

"And the helicopter?" Okudaira asked.

"The pilot, copilot and gunner are on board. They have night-vision equipment as well, but we stayed to the shadows and cover. They made no indication of noticing us."

"Why would that aircraft be parked there?" the Yakuza boss asked.

"They appear to be waiting for something. They have powered their craft down," Kenji said. "We have them surrounded."

Okudaira frowned. "Take the helicopter quickly. I want you to interrogate the crew and find out what happened."

Kenji nodded and disappeared into the shadows.

DARKNESS HAD ENVELOPED the valley entirely, and the trek to reach the base of the cliff was a long and difficult one. Honey limped along weakly, helped by two of Machida's men, who kept her from stumbling more than once when her feet gave out under her.

"Shouldn't we have left her back at the blind spot?" Machida asked Bolan softly.

The Executioner shook his head. "I want her close to the base."

Machida studied the big American's face in the dim moonlight, then nodded. "If my men make a move to abduct her while we're in the base…"

"She'll make enough noise to wake the dead," Bolan answered. "It'll get you and me killed for certain."

"And bring down a swarm of guards on them," Machida finished. "A shrewd plan. But of course, this means Honey herself would be killed in the following conflagration."

"She was willing to risk being shot in the back before," Bolan said. "And if she ends up back in captivity, she'll be in worse danger than before."

Machida frowned. "I would allow no harm to befall her."

Bolan nodded. "I guessed that."

"You read me as an honorable man?" Machida asked.

"Honey was willing to make a deal with you. As for me, I do know you left Hogan to rot."

"He was a barbarian," Machida answered.

Bolan nodded. "Yeah. I dealt with him too. Better that you got in the first move before he got the drop on you."

"He wasn't happy that you bested his efforts to ambush you."

Bolan shrugged. "I disappoint lots of people. It's an occupational hazard for me."

"That's funny. I would have thought all the bullets and blades would be the worse hazard," Machida said, smiling.

"There's that too, but that doesn't hurt my feelings as much," Bolan returned.

Machida managed a soft chuckle. Bolan took a deep breath. He was allowing himself to get friendly with the mobster. This was a man he'd sworn to protect Honey Anthony from. If the time came to engage in brutal combat against him, the distraction of knowing Machida as a man of honor, a man of humor, could slow him.

Bolan steeled himself.

He didn't particularly like the prospect of battling the Yakuza man.

They approached the great black jutting cliffside. Only a smattering of light spilled from under the camouflage netting covering the base facility. In the shadow of the mountain, there was hardly any natural light from the clear, starlit sky.

Silence came over the men. Bolan's muscles warmed now, their aches and pains disappearing in a flush of adrenaline. Strength flowed through his limbs, as sure and steady as ever. He knew that he would pay for it later, when he came down off the adrenal rush, but for the moment, he was able to fight again. His mind was clear and sharp, his eyes adjusting to the dim light.

He cinched the submachine gun tightly across his back. For the penetration, he would require stealth. Bolan had accumulated several knives from the dead Black Serpents. The sword would be for up close, but without a silenced weapon, he would have to resort to throwing the blades. He didn't like the idea of using throwing knives, but it was his best ranged option.

But desperate times called for desperate measures, and the Executioner had learned improvisation through necessity. He could turn an empty revolver into a skull-crushing throwing iron, a bowl of boiling noodles into a weapon that could disarm a submachine-gun wielding thug, and he'd learned how to sink six inches of blade into the heart of a man at six yards. In the Executioner's many battles, Bolan had transformed simple items into weapons of survival.

It was the same with men like Machida, men with whom he'd entered into fragile, uneasy alliances. He made do with what he had. He found allies where he could. Certainly, Machida would be ready for the opportunity, the slim, split-second opening where he could make his own move. And when the Japanese gangster did, because Bolan knew that he couldn't remain on guard against his ally at all times, the Executioner would have the scarcest of heartbeats to react.

Mack Bolan would not give up. Not with the Black Serpents up to deadly schemes, a plot nearing fruition that would make the Tokyo subway nerve gas attacks seem like a mere scratch on the surface of a great city. Lord Zakoji, whoever he truly was, was the threat of the hour, the menace that stood looming not over a single innocent girl's life, not even over his own life and the lives of a few ragtag surviving gangsters. Zakoji was a fury that was going to be unleashed against untold numbers of helpless, unknowing lives. Men, women and children of all walks of life were the target of the Burakku Uwibami cult leader in order to shatter modern Japan and remold the pieces back into something that he considered his ideal nation.

The Yakuza were still villains, racketeers, extortionists, drug dealers, and stone cold killers, but they had not gotten to their level of power by indiscriminately harming the Japanese populace. In this instance, Bolan had chosen the lesser evil to side with. One smaller beast, to side with against the great Black Serpents.

Bolan paused. Something was wrong, and it wasn't Machida or his Yakuza men. Sure, the Executioner had steered them quietly away from one patrol that stumbled in their direction, keeping away from conflict that would attract undue attention. But Bolan sensed something else was out, stalking.

It wasn't a psychic sense, per se, but there was something that his subconscious mind was detecting, but his own conscious senses weren't able to focus on. An uneasy feeling, perhaps a wrong rustle of leaves, the scent of something wafting in the breeze, or an odd shadow that fell at the edge of his peripheral vision.

Of course, he knew that if Hogan had brought in three helicopters, he would have a few extra men, and he would be on the hunt, even in the dark, for the Anthony girl. And then Bolan realized what the unease was.

"Machida?" Bolan asked, stopping the group, but keeping close, careful watch.

"What is it?" the Yakuza boss asked.

"The blueprints...did Hogan take them with him when you were attacked at the clearing?"

Machida furrowed his brow, struggling to remember.

"No. We never even got the blueprints out," Machida answered.

Bolan nodded. He hadn't seen them when he'd accompanied the mercenaries, so that meant that they might have hidden the blueprints away. However, the Black Serpents, even if they were fanatics, were not stupid. They would have made a point of searching the vehicles. There was a chance that they might have found the blueprints.

There was no time now to head back and check, and even if they did, there was no guaruntee that they wouldn't stumble across a dozen more patrols, or worse, Hogan's men trying to secure the vehicles themselves, searching for the blueprints. The Executioner's gut twisted.

"What were the blueprints?" Bolan asked.

Machida frowned. "Okudaira knew for certain. He just told me that they were worth twenty girls like Rebecca."

Bolan glanced toward Honey. "No paper is worth a human life."

Machida nodded. "I agree. But from what little I do know of those blueprints, they could cost hundreds of lives."

Bolan set his jaw. "And that why you're willing to risk your own?"

"It's hard to conduct business in a city destroyed by a madman with a billionare arms designer's most potent weaponry," Machida said. He shrugged. "Plus, that's where I keep all my belongings."

Bolan almost managed a smile. "All right. You're coming with me. The fewer in the infiltration, the better, but…"

"But you'd like some collatoral."

Bolan nodded. "And backup."

Machida nodded back. "All right."

"We'll keep an eye out for the blueprints and take care of them once we find them," Bolan said.

"Take care of them?" Machida asked.

"Do you really want to sell Anthony's technology to terrorists?"

Machida shook his head. "This whole affair leaves a bitter taste in my mouth. Okudaira is newly in power, and his plots…kidnapping, black market…"

"You've lost too many of your men because of this," Bolan said.

"That's correct. And the longer he tries to run things his way… We were never saints before. I'm not going to lie about that. But gambling and smuggling contraband is not the same as bargaining with terrorists," Machida responded.

Bolan pursed his lips. He decided to play a gambit card. "I intended to use the Anthony kidnapping to get me closer to your boss."

"To deal with him?" Machida asked.

"He wants to expand into business that can do a lot of people harm. And if he's not stopped, there will be suffering," Bolan stated. "I intended to remove him."

Machida's eyes narrowed. "So you're not an FBI agent."

"That's what the badge says," the Executioner answered.

Machida nodded slowly. "I have my duty to my organization, Cooper."

Bolan stiffened some.

"And while you might think that's blind obedience, in truth, it means I am devoted to making sure it has the best leadership possible," Machida said.

"I understand," Bolan told him softly.

Still, the Executioner kept an eye on the Yakuza leader. Just in case he wasn't telling the truth, though for everyone's sake, Bolan hoped that Machida was.

KENJI CROUCHED at the tree line, his night-vision goggles casting the world in a hazy, eerie green hue. Shapes moved in the confines of the Bell LongRanger helicopter parked in the middle of the clearing. The pilot and copilot were shifting, trying to find a comfortable seating position, while the door gunner pivoted left and right.

The helicopter crew was on edge, and Kenji's job was to take them all, or as many as he could, alive and kicking. He knew that the door gunner was the most dangerous of the trio, but the pilot and copilot could cause trouble if they were in communication with other forces.

Kenji glided out of his position, keeping low and in a crouch. He was dressed head to toe in black. He patterned himself after the United States Navy SEALs in their night operations gear. Basic black was impressive, and it matched his very black military weapons, from his phosphate-bladed, synthetic handled Kraton knife to his all black, silenced MP-5.

Kenji had briefed his men in the takedown of the helicopter crew. They were to be taken alive, if at all possible. Okudaira wanted them interrogated.

Crawling slowly, across the black gravel, Kenji pulled himself into position to cover the doorgunner.

From the rear, two more of Kenji's men moved softly, their boots not disturbing the stones they stepped across, planning to hit the helicopter from the other side. If necessary, Kenji would core the door gunner, because the M-249 Squad Automatic Weapon in his hands was enough to rouse the entire valley once it went off.

The door gunner twitched and spun his weapon toward the tree line behind Kenji. The Yakuza soldier stayed very still, not even daring to lower his head, because that much movement would register on the night-vision goggles of the mercenary.

Caught out in the open, Kenji was vulnerable if the door gunner could make out his still form against the black rocks beneath him. Only by being rigid and immobile could he avoid attracting deadly attention to himself. All it would take would be a flexing of the gunner's finger, and Kenji's body would be torn to shreds by a point-blank blast of slugs.

Slowly, he adjusted the aim of his weapon toward the door gunner, keeping his motion subtle, barely noticable. The fat muzzle of his sound-suppressed MP-5 edged toward the mercenary. Each degree, each inch closer to the machine gun-toting killer in the door was a victory earned through aching muscles and cold sweat.

Finally, the muzzle was pointed at his target. The front sight was a fuzzy black ring in his vision, circling the torso of the enemy gunman.

Kenji saw the shapes of his men reach the other side of the helicopter, rushing like the shadows of predators. The pilot was suddenly yanked through his door and thrown to the ground, stones clattering. The door gunner turned at the sound, trying to swing the length of his big machine gun around in the tight confines of the Bell helicopter's cabin. As he struggled with the snagged barrel, Kenji jumped to his feet, charging.

The mercenary gunner caught the movement out of the corner of his eye, and swung his muzzle back toward Kenji, but by the time be brought the weapon to bear, the powerful Japanese gangster was on him, his weight tossing aside the crewman's aim. With a savage yank, Kenji twisted the SAW out of his enemy's hands, the trigger finger of the gunner snapping as it snagged in the trigger guard. The mercenary gave a howl of pain, but Kenji swung the buttstock of his machine pistol, smashing the man in the face. Bones cracked under the wicked impact, and the gunner slumped to the floor of the helicopter.

Kenji reversed his submachine gun and aimed it at the gunner.

"Stay still, and you live for a little while," the Yakuza enforcer growled.

The mercenary was too dazed to struggle.

Now, it was time to get answers.

Kenji pulled out his knife.

"Open up and tell me everything...."

THE FENCE HAD NO SENSORS on it. Bolan had made sure of that by double and triple checking it. And luckily, there was no electrical current running through it, either. But there were cameras. His eyes, adjusted to the darkness, picked out five of them, and he sat, studying their arc of vision and the timing of their rotation.

It would be difficult, but not impossible. He dug his fingers under the chain links and pulled up hard.

"Go through and wait for me," Bolan said to Machida.

Machida shoved his gear through and scurried under the fence. His borrowed body armor snagged on the bottom links, but he ripped himself free and got to his feet. He turned back, grabbed the fence and held it for Bolan.

Bolan was taller, and more powerfully built than Machida, but after he'd gotten his shoulders through, the taper of his chest down to his narrow waist and hips helped him slide through faster. He stood up and glanced around as Machida let the chain links down slowly.

"Step where I step," Bolan whispered.

Machida nodded. "Cameras."

"At the very least," Bolan answered. "If there are any motion detectors, we're in trouble."

"But you don't think they have motion detectors here?" Machida asked.

Bolan scanned the ground one more time. "Too much activity in the camp. It would create seismic clutter."

"Which is why we were able to slip past the patrols," Machida surmised.

Bolan nodded, then put his finger to his lips.

He drew the katana and, using his memorized layout of the cameras, stepped off into the shadows, Machida on his heels.

RHODES HOGAN led the four-man stick of mercenaries through the darkness. He'd managed to get some medical treatment in the helicopter, tended to by Sinclair, and had a fresh change of clothing. The mud and sweat were peeled off and replaced with a crisp new battle dress uniform, a new submachine gun and pistol, and he was feeling better. He hadn't had a chance to rest much, but his strength had returned and he felt refreshed by being clean.

As he approached the cliff, he flipped a pair of night-vision goggles over his eyes. Enemy patrols strolled the paths leading to the secret base, and Hogan crouched deeply. His four mercenaries spread out and took cover in the foliage. Hogan, obscured by shrubbery, could see that some of the Black Serpent sentries were equipped with their own night-vision goggles.

Maybe it was because of a lack of funds for enough goggles, or maybe it was because the sentries had appropriated gear from Hogan's own mercenaries. Whatever the case, the men were organized enough so that each patrol had at least one man among them with a set of night-vision devices scanning the woods.

Night vision, however, was not able to pierce the thickness of foliage, and even if some parts of Hogan were visible through gaps in the leaves, in the green, hazy mottling of the digitally enhanced images, he knew there was not enough contrast. He simply blended into the darkness.

Though it was tempting to begin weeding out the opposition, and not have enemy soldiers at his back, there was too much of a chance that these men were in communication with the main base. Sure enough, he saw one Black Serpent raise a hand radio to his lips, whispering imperceptably into the microphone. A soft hiss of static returned, and the sentry nodded as he listened.

Taking out the patrols would be a waste of precious ammunition, as well as serving to alert the black-clad cultists to the presence of the mercenary force.

Hogan lowered his gun, then nodded to his fellow mercs to do the same.

There would be no taking out the enemy yet. There was no need to create martyrs.

More importantly, Hogan observed, there was no sign of Cooper, nor Machida. They were not here, at least not this far out on the perimeter. Hogan wondered, idly, if maybe the two men hadn't formed an alliance. If they did, it would make things a little more difficult for him. Hogan had enough men to take back the blueprints, and take out a single man, even one as talented as Cooper. However, dealing with more than just Cooper would be suicide.

They were pushing themselves to the limits. The probe into

the cult base would be one of the most dangerous operations Hogan had ever undertaken. He usually liked to go in with overwhelming force, though he was good at stealth and tracking when he needed to be.

As the patrol turned the corner of the path, Hogan slid from his hiding space and led his crew closer to the enemy installation.

The blueprints were vital. If he found Rebecca Anthony, so much the better.

And, if he had his way, Cooper would accidentally step in front of a stream of Parabellum slugs.

The fence of the compound loomed ahead and Hogan crouched low. He scanned the perimeter and saw that it was kept dimly lit. He shouldered his submachine gun, allowing the scope mounted on top to cut the distances involved.

He didn't want to touch the fence and light up some kind of perimeter alarm, or worse, set off an electrified fence. There was also the possibility of on-base cameras to consider.

Sure enough, in Hogan's initial pass, he spotted three cameras. He knew there could have been a half-dozen more in well-hidden places.

Getting close would be tight and dangerous.

Hogan swept the base grounds again, suddenly seeing the familiar, tall form of Agent Matt Cooper stalking in the shadows. Hogan crouched deeper on instinct, almost in fear of the sudden appearance of the big stranger.

Of course, Cooper couldn't resist cutting in on the mysterious little organization's headquarters. He might even have been trying to find the blueprints.

If Cooper was around, Hogan knew that meant that the Anthony girl could be nearby.

Hogan froze, catching the sight of a familiar set of Japanese features.

It was Machida.

Hogan cursed the Yakuza bastard and cursed himself for not killing him as soon as he had the chance.

But now, Hogan thought with a smile, he had that chance.

He just had to let Cooper and Machida do all the work of finding the blueprints.

## 14

With Machida following in his footsteps, the Executioner, katana drawn, padded silently, keeping to the shadows. His back was against the wall out of the view of the remote cameras dotting the compound.

If they got into a conflict, Bolan knew that the image of a dead sentry picked up by the cameras would throw the whole compound into an alert. Quiet kills would still leave behind evidence.

Bolan froze and heard the hiss of a radio and a low murmured voice answering the call. He looked back to Machida, but the Yakuza man's ears were sharp, and he was pressed tight against the wall of a prefab building right next to him. Machida shrugged, wanting to know the Executioner's next move. Bolan put his finger to his lips. Machida nodded and they let the sentry continue to talk.

Bolan remained tense. The conversation continued, but the Executioner could see that Machida was listening intently.

The sentry took a couple of steps forward, and Bolan could make out the black shadow of his form. On his waist was a kami, and over one shoulder was strapped a submachine gun. The Black Serpent guard looked left, then right, but thankfully not over his shoulder, and then took off toward the fence.

"What was said?" Bolan whispered.

"He was just reporting in that everything was quiet. There was some excitement though, earlier," Machida said. "He was being told about the death of one of the mercenaries at the sword of Lord Zakoji."

"A sword fight?" Bolan asked.

"The details were sketchy, but it seemed that the mercenary didn't want to be part of the testing going on."

Bolan frowned. "Zakoji's biological weapon."

Machida nodded. "The dispatcher said the dead mercenary saw what happened to his friend and tried to make a break for it. He grabbed a sword, but Zakoji carved him to ribbons."

"Then Zakoji must have his weapon perfected, or nearly perfected, "Bolan said. "We have to stop him tonight."

Machida nodded. "I agree."

Bolan scanned around the corner, keeping his face close to the wall, exposing only a small sliver of himself to see the layout in the next area. The main building had two cameras at the corners. They were mounted and arced so that one watched the front at all times.

That was okay. Bolan wasn't going for the front door. He didn't have a view of the side of the building.

Bolan waved for Machida to head back, then slipped around the Yakuza enforcer. The Executioner went to the corner and again, surveyed the side of the building. There was a single camera mounted, facing a side entrance. This one did not swivel like the units watching the front.

The camera mounting was low enough and appeared sturdy enough for a tall man to boost another person on top of it and over the short subroof to get to the top of the building. He could also move outside the visual range of the single camera. It would require a bit of weaving to avoid detection, but they would be able to climb up in the blind spot.

He nodded to Machida, and the Yakuza man gave him a thumbs-up.

Whatever the Executioner planned, he was ready for it.

The two men moved off into the darkness.

UNNO'S FACE HURT, BUT NOT so badly anymore. The man who had laid open his flesh with the frame of the submachine gun had even helped to tend to the cut. The Yakuza gunman didn't believe that Cooper did it out of kindness, but out of practicality.

However, Unno had respect for that.

He could have feigned a lack of knowledge with dealing with injuries. Instead, using moisture squeezed from leaves, Cooper had washed out the serious cut, and used several strips of electrical tape they'd found on one of their dead enemies. He'd even closed the wound and sealed it off from further infection.

Unno's fury at the man had abated, and he'd quickly recognized the sense of Machida's seeking an alliance with Cooper. Initially, Unno had unvoiced concerns about allying themselves with an enemy who had sliced through their ranks like wheat, but now, with the big American on their side, for the first time, Unno felt as if he had a chance of making it out of this valley alive.

Something moved in the bushes, and Unno spun, bringing his Uzi around. He dared not pull the trigger on the unsilenced weapon. The rattle of an automatic weapon would shatter any shred of stealth and secrecy that Cooper and Machida had on their side in their penetration of the Black Serpent compound.

Still, if it came to survival, he was going to do what he had to and fire his weapon to protect himself. He only hoped that Machida and Cooper would welcome the distraction.

The other Yakuza men saw Unno's reaction to the subdued

sound and got to their feet. Their eyes were wide with fear. They, too, knew that getting into a gunfight would only bring down the wrath of the Black Serpents, their patrols already having passed close to their hiding spot.

Honey Anthony had her pistol locked in her hand. While she was not frightened of the Yakuza men anymore, she too sensed something was wrong. Her hands shook, and Unno stood closer to her.

"It's okay, little one," the Yakuza gunman told her softly.

Honey's clear blue eyes flashed nervously to him, and while her knuckles were white around the handle of her handgun, she nodded in agreement at his reassuring words.

Honey's eyes swept the surrounding foliage, full of the shapes of branches and leaves moving in the slight breeze, but also full of hidden monsters and terrors. Unno saw her furrowed brow and grim frown. Her jaw flexed, tensed tightly, nostrils flaring.

If his face hadn't hurt still, Unno would have spared a moment for a smile. The girl had recovered from her fear and nervousness, replacing it with anger and intense focus. She might not have been a gunfighter, but she still had fire and willingness to fight.

That might be just enough to get her through this. Unno hoped so.

He regretted having been involved in her kidnapping. She was close to his age, and he had seen her around the Tokyo clubs late at night. Indeed, it was his best friend, left slain on a hillside in this same forsaken valley, who had passed on the information to Okudaira, their boss. Unno's gut churned, and he regretted being dragged into the deadly situation.

He thought the current head of their gangster clan was full of shit, and worth tossing aside in favor of a man with honor and respect, like Machida.

He shook himself out of his daydreams and focused on the danger at hand. Once again tense and ready to go, Unno whipped around when he heard the meaty slap of a bullet striking flesh. There was no sound of a gunshot, but one of the other Yakuza gunmen went down, his face blasted to a gory pit of shattered skull and brains. Unno grabbed Honey and pushed her to the ground, aiming his Uzi at the darkness. Still he held his fire, not having a decent target.

Another Yakuza gunman spun, gurgling as his hand went to his throat. A fountain of blood leaked through his fingers. He slumped against a tree, trying to suck in breath. Bubbles and streams of crimson foamed from the corners of his mouth.

Unno couldn't hold back any longer and he held down the trigger on the Uzi, sweeping the bushes. The rattle and thunder of the machine pistol crashed through the darkness, rumbling freely and alerting the whole valley to their presence.

There was no way for them to protect themselves otherwise.

Something plucked at Unno's shoulder, hot pain flaring from the gunshot wound. He staggered but held his ground over Honey.

"Stay down!" Unno yelled to the girl, but even prone, she was firing her pistol into the shadows. He tried to fumble for a magazine, but the fingers of his left hand had gone numb from the impact of the enemy bullet. His gun was empty, and he was still under attack.

Something came out of nowhere, smashing Unno in the head and throwing him to the ground.

"Unno!" he heard Honey screech. The Yakuza man tried to move, but his whole body had gone numb. His eyes were clear, however, despite the hot splash of blood coating his face. He struggled to move, but his limbs weren't responding. His heart hammered, but his breathing was steady and even.

Was he dying? Did the bullet smash his brains to pudding? He worked his lips, but no words came out.

Shapes loomed out of the shadows, and one rushed up to grab Honey as she crouched over him. The girl's eyes met Unno's, and then she looked away.

"You killed him!" she screeched, then kicked a man in the hip. "You miserable bastards!"

"Shut up!" Hogan snarled and backhanded her across the face. "Let's clear out of here, now!"

Unno stayed still, his eyes looking up through the canopy of trees, seeing the twinkle of stars up above. He cursed. He would have loved to come up with a new plan, other than playing possum for the second time that day, but the jolt of the bullet against his cranium rendered anything more complicated than laying comatose a moot point. The sound of rushing feet faded, and Unno felt his finger twitch. He struggled to close his hand into a fist, but it seemingly took forever. More racing feet pounded, and the stunned Yakuza man was too immobilized to even flinch.

Three Black Serpents raced past him, hurtling into the darkness after Hogan and Honey. One man stopped and looked at the corpses of the Yakuza men.

"Forget them! Get the intruders!" one of the other Black Serpents shouted.

The sentry stood over Unno, looking down into his staring eyes. Unno couldn't even blink, but he held his breath.

"I said come on!" the Black Serpent snapped.

The guard looming over Unno shrugged and continued on into the darkness.

Suddenly Unno's fingers snapped shut, closing into a fist. His eyes blinked. Breath sucked raggedly into his lungs.

Unno lurched, sitting upright. His shoulder hurt, but it was nothing compared to his headache. The bullet had to have only glanced off his skull, but it had been enough to leave him dazed for several moments.

Unno caught his breath, waiting for his head to stop throbbing. The Black Serpents had raced through and hadn't taken any of the guns from the dead Yakuza enforcers, and he felt grateful for that. He patted around for the gun he'd dropped when he had been shot. The electrical tape on his cheek peeled away from his skin, loosened by the dripping blood. He reloaded the submachine gun and staggered to his feet.

Three more of his Yakuza companions were gone, slaughtered by Hogan's men.

And Honey was captured again.

Unno took a tenative step. His head pounded with pain where the bullet glanced off it.

But he was armed again.

And he'd sworn to Machida and Cooper that he would protect Honey.

He wouldn't let those three down.

AS MACHIDA HELPED Bolan crawl onto the roof over the camera, they heard the blast of Uzi fire.

Fear cut through Machida's features, and the Executioner's face hardened with concern.

They looked at each other, weighing the implications of the gunfire.

"Were they discovered?" Machida asked.

"Even if they were, there's nothing we can do now," Bolan answered.

Machida started to say something, but he read the conflict in his companion's face.

"We have to stop Zakoji and hope Honey and the others are safe," Bolan said.

Machida nodded numbly, then gripped his submachine

gun tighter. Bolan advanced to the window, making sure he wouldn't be seen.

The office was ornate, with a giant red silk tapestry of a huge, coiled black serpent looming over modern-day Tokyo. In one corner was a stand for a pair of katanas, painted black, matching the simple, tasteful black sheath and handle of the one sword sitting on the display. The other was gone, presumably with its Zakoji. Bolan tried the window, but it was locked.

Bolan looked at the window frame and the glass and spotted a small strip of copper lining the frame. He took one of his knives and looked in the reflection of the blade at where the metallic strip disappeared between the upper and lower windows. The copper was connected to another layer of metal and would undoubtedly set off an alarm if opened. However, through the glass, Bolan could hear the sound of alarm bells going off in the wake of the gunfire outside of the perimeter.

Taking a chance, he jammed the blade into the frame. It took some effort, grinding through the aluminum and the rubber seal. Finally he dislodged the two locks. Bolan pushed open the window and slid into the office, sword drawn. The sound of the alarms had not changed with the opening of the window.

On the desk was a set of blueprints, held open with paperweights. The Executioner didn't have to look at them to know what they were. Anthony's Ironworks emblem showed in the corner of the papers. Bolan stepped closer and looked them over, his blood chilling.

They were designs for a Global-Positioning-System-guided surface-to-surface long-range missile system. The range was only eight hundred miles, not that long for artillery missiles, but according to the specifications for the rocket motor, they would be able to launch faster than anything most missile defense cannons could stop.

In the warhead compartment of the missiles was space for a variety of payloads, including biological and chemical shells.

Bolan didn't want to think of the capabilities of this missile in the hands of terrorists armed with Anthrax, or sarin gas. The fact that the missiles were also highly portable and required little effort or preparation to launch made them ideal for either motorized infantry in need of artillery support, or most chillingly, a terrorist operation with a simple truck.

Machida looked at Bolan for a moment but continued to watch the door to the office.

"What's wrong?" Machida whispered.

"Okudaira's payment was for a high-tech, medium-range artillery missile system," Bolan answered. The more he read of the missile's capabilities, the less he liked it. Equipped with terrain-reading radar, the missiles could travel safely, and swiftly at an altitude of twelve feet, far below radar, hugging canyons, forests, or city streets with equal ease, until their GPS brought them to a pinpoint location, right on target.

Then, whatever the payload, the warhead would detonate.

Even armed with conventional warheads, the Ironworks weapons would have the capability of blowing the lower floors of a skyscraper into shattered wreckage, turning the building into a death trap for thousands of people trapped on the upper floors. One of them, slamming into the lobby of a building like the Sears Tower or the Empire State Building would create thousand-foot-tall coffins of collapsing steel and glass for anyone not killed by the initial blast.

"What do you mean?" Machida asked.

"The missiles that Okudaira intended to put on the black market would turn cities into blazing death traps for anyone able to get within eight hundred miles of them," Bolan told him.

Machida swallowed hard. "That doesn't narrow it down much."

"Terrorists, armed with these, would be unstoppable."

The Executioner grabbed the blueprints.

"Tear them into pieces," Machida said.

Bolan tilted his head.

"Tear them into pieces. Shuffle them and give half to me. This way, if one of us is captured or killed—" Machida said.

"They won't have anything but disorganized scraps to work from," Bolan finished. He immediately began shredding the blueprints in his hands, ripping them into smaller handfuls.

He shuffled the mess on the desk, then scooped one wad of papers and stuffed them into a pocket on his body-armor vest. He grabbed another handful and passed them to Machida.

Machida stuffed them in one of his pockets, then gave Bolan a curt nod.

The doorknob twisted. The two men looked at it, standing stock-still, eyes wide.

Their time was runing out. The minute the door cracked open, the Black Serpents would know that they had been invaded.

The Executioner drew his katana, bringing it up in a deadly arc.

RHODE HOGAN CURSED. One of his four mercenaries was down. He'd hoped to keep it quiet, using silenced weapons to take Rebecca Anthony stealthily. Instead, it turned into a blazing firefight, the forest coming alive in a slithering nest of Black Serpents.

Honey twisted and fought against Hogan's grip.

"Let me go!" she snarled.

Hogan turned and slapped her hard. She coughed and sputtered, still pulling to get her arm away from the mercenary. Hogan yanked her off her feet and leveled the muzzle of his machine pistol at her head.

"Stop fucking around with me, bitch!" Hogan snarled.

"Go ahead and do it!" Honey snapped. "The only thing you'll get is an assload of lead when Cooper finishes with you!"

Rage reddened the rims of Honey's clear blue eyes, and for a moment, Hogan took a step backwards. His finger flexed against the trigger, and he would have gone through with it, but he realized that he needed a bargaining chip. Instead, he signaled to one of his men.

"Pick this stupid bitch up," Hogan growled. "If I touch her again, I'll kill her."

One of the mercenaries rushed forward and scooped up the slight girl, throwing her over his shoulder. The merc chuckled and gave the stunned Honey a slap on the ass. Hogan almost laughed, then he felt a 9 mm bullet slam into the chest of his body armor.

"Get moving!" Hogan snapped, leveling his weapon and cutting loose with a burst into the trees. A man screamed out in Japanese from the shadows, and the mercenaries took off in a quick run, looking to put more distance between themselves and the Black Serpents.

More sporadic gunfire chased them, and Hogan ducked his head. Tree trunks splintered as bullets hammered into them. All around him, storms of automatic fire chased through the woods.

Static burst over Hogan's earpiece. "Hogan! Dammit, Hogan, we're under fire!"

"Sinclair?" Hogan asked. He slowed, but a bullet smacking his armor made him pick up his pace again. The helicopter had dropped Sinclair back at the other two birds after they assembled as many men as they could for this penetration. Hogan preferred to keep his second in command at the rear.

He wanted a capable leader able to back him up if he got in trouble.

Now the sound of machine gun fire rattled over Hogan's radio. Suddenly, in the distance, he heard the hollow thumps of explosions. The sky flared briefly with the lightning of detonating helicopters.

Hogan watched, slack jawed as two aircraft were blown to smithereens. Underlit, their third helicopter turned and swooped across the valley.

Things were turning to shit fast.

"Rikyu!"

The Black Serpent reacted to the sound of his master's voice instantly, rushing to his side.

"There's gunfire outside of the compound," Zakoji told him.

"Sir, I shall lead—"

"You will do nothing," Zakoji said, cutting him off. "Get to my office and bring me the blueprints from my desk."

Rikyu nodded. "But—"

"We have enough guards on the perimeter to deal with whatever incursion is coming in. But it might be a feint, a distraction," Zakoji explained. "I do not want my new blueprints taken from me."

Rikyu's eyebrows went up with realization. "They could be trying to break into our compound. Yes, Master. I shall get the blueprints immediately."

Zakoji glared at the Black Serpent lieutenant who turned and raced up the stairs. Rikyu reached for the door and turned the knob.

As he entered the office, he saw two men. Both were

dressed in black body armor, holding swords. For a moment, confusion reigned in the Black Serpent's mind. Then the larger man flashed forward.

There was a brief sting of pain as Rikyu stood there. The sword disappeared, and he wondered where it went. He lowered his gaze, and saw that there was a crimson fissure down the center of his chest. Rikyu took a deep breath, and as his chest expanded, the fissure split, a geyser of blood pouring from the wound.

Darkness descended on Rikyu as rough hands grabbed him and hauled him into the office.

MACHIDA CAUGHT the slumped corpse of the man who'd entered the office. Bolan's sword stroke had been instantly effective, cutting off the man's cry before he could alert the others. However, he'd been sent up to the office for a purpose. Chances were, someone would be coming up to check on him if he didn't come back soon. Bolan had only bought them moments of breathing space.

It would have to be enough.

"Which way now?" Machida asked.

Bolan peered through the door. It was cracked a tiny bit, and he surveyed the stairs. A man in long robes with an ornate, embroidered serpent decorating his chest was pacing, giving orders. The sword on his belt, one that matched the one on the display stand, identified him as a Zakoji.

The Black Serpents were all a flutter. Most were armed only with handguns, though racks of submachine guns and rifles were placed sporadically around the room. All it would take would be one pull of the trigger on his Uzi. Of course, that would do nothing to the stored weapons that the madman was harboring, and the other Black Serpents would sweep up the steps, guns blazing.

Bolan frowned. There were no weapons in the office but the katana and, while the Uzi was a good gun, it couldn't lay down the sheer levels of devastation needed to turn the cult's headquarters, and the dozens of men below, into a shattered battle zone. A grenade launcher would have been ideal right, especially to take out the racks of automatic weapons stored at the base of the stairs.

Bolan sheathed his sword and pulled out his Uzi and SIG-Sauer.

"What are you doing?" Machida asked.

"Get out of the building. See if you can find Honey and the others," Bolan said. "If they're still alive."

Machida frowned. "And you'll deal with the Black Serpents yourself?"

"Yeah," Bolan said. "I don't want to risk your life, or have your half of the shreds of the blueprints fall back into their hands."

Machida looked back to the window. Bolan could tell that the Yakuza man was torn.

"I'll do what damage I can," Bolan said. "I'm not going to try anything suicidal."

"Cooper, you're good, but there's a swarm of those Black Serpents down there. The minute you stop to reload, they'll be all over you," Machida answered.

Bolan looked around the office, trying to find something to provide some kind of advantage. He spotted a lantern on the desk. It was a paper lantern, with a candle inside. If it had oil in it, it might provide a flash fire when it crashed against something.

He looked down into it and saw a wick sticking out of a cup of oil. Not enough, though. It would only make a small splash. But it did give Bolan an idea. He started going through Zakoji's desk drawers, and found a container for replenishing the oil in the lantern. He gave it a shake.

There was oil in the can, but it wouldn't do much more than to make a slightly larger splash. No, it wasn't going to match the destructive power of a thermite grenade. But, maybe, if Bolan found something else....

The square frame of the oiled paper lantern looked large enough to pour out the contents of the oil flask, with room to spare. Bolan needed something more.

"Give me the shreds from your part of the blueprints," he told Machida.

Machida raised an eyebrow, then saw the oil that Bolan had.

"I'm going to use the papers," Bolan told him. He pulled his borrowed shirt out of his waistband and tore a long strip of cloth that he soaked down with oil. Wadding up the blueprints, he poured more oil over them. A piece of copy paper with a hole punched into it for the wick, and some of Zakoji's tape, and his improvised firebomb was ready. He took a lighter from Zakoji's desk and checked it to make sure that it sparked to flame immediately.

"Do you think you can take someone out with that?" Machida asked.

Bolan frowned. He had a weapon. Now for a perfect target.

"The gun racks," he said quickly.

"The flames will keep them from grabbing automatic weapons," Machida answered.

"Get ready to throw open the door," Bolan told him.

Machida moved to the doorway.

At that moment, the door slammed open, clipping the Yakuza man in the shoulder. Zakoji snarled in Japanese as he bulled through the doorway, followed by three men, then froze, standing face-to-face with the Executioner.

Bolan's mastery of Japanese was far from complete. But

the intent of Zakoji's subsequent command would have been clear in any language.

*"Kill him!"*

**15**

In hot pursuit of Hogan and Honey, Unno raced through the woods, his head pounding as hard as his heart. He'd been hit too hard over the past twenty-four hours, and his strength was starting to fail him, but he kept going, pushing one foot in front of the other. He wasn't about to let down Machida and didn't want to fail Cooper or Honey, either. Cooper had done too much to help them after they hooked up with the big American. Honey didn't have to trust them or convince Cooper that working with the few Yakuza survivors was for all their good, but she had.

Cooper didn't have to clean his wounds. He didn't have to risk his life to stop a madman's terror rampage against an entire city, the city that Unno had grown up in. Even though he was a criminal, he loved Tokyo. It was his home, it was where he lived, ate, and slept. He had a love for the city even if he was scurrying in its back alleys, facing down other gangsters and thugs, struggling to carve out a life in its underbelly.

He caught up with a pair of Black Serpents who were scrambling between trees. Unno raised his Uzi and triggered it, blasting one of the cultists in the upper back. The recoil walked a line of bullets into the base of the gunman's skull and pitched him forward. As the first cultist tumbled lifelessly, the other spun and opened fire.

Unno was knocked back, stunned by the force of enemy slugs hammering his body armor. Somehow, the Yakuza enforcer managed to hold his ground and swept the other man at thigh level. The body armor didn't extend that far down, and Unno was rewarded as the Black Serpent was thrown off his feet, screaming as he slammed into the ground.

Unno rushed forward and stomped hard on the wounded man's neck. A brutal snap sounded. The Black Serpent sentry shuddered, then went still. Unno's ankle hurt from the jarring impact with the dead man's spine, but he continued hobbling along.

Gunfire chattered ahead, and he knew that Hogan and the Black Serpent patrols were trading automatic fire. His heart sunk as he thought of Honey, caught in the cross fire, and he ran faster, ignoring the painful protests of his ankle.

MACHIDA SAW BOLAN, both of his hands full with the lantern and the lighter. He lunged into action and threw his body across the path of the three men that Zakoji had sent charging toward him. The Yakuza man grunted as he felt the trio slam into him, and all of them were tossed to the floor in a tangle of limbs.

Bolan released the objects in his hands, and before gravity could even take hold of them, launched himself like a harpoon, catching Zakoji in the chest and bowling him backward into the hallway at the top of the stairs. With a crash, the two men splintered the railing, almost snapping through it.

Zakoji snarled with feral rage, hammering Bolan in the jaw with a palm strike that rocked the Executioner's head. The big American hooked his foot hard into Zakoji's kidney, the punched him in the upper chest, where his clavicle met his breastbone. The cult leader flipped back over the broken rail, screaming as he hit the floor twelve feet below.

Bolan spun and grabbed a Black Serpent who was rising to his feet after Machida had knocked him down. He then swung the smaller man in front of him like a shield. Other cultists recovered their senses and reacted to the sudden violence at the top of the stairs. Huddling behind the smaller man, Bolan unslung his Uzi with one sure motion. Bullets smashed into his human shield, making the helpless Black Serpent jerk spastically.

One of Machida's other wrestling partners lurched, rising to a half-crouch. He cocked one fist to hammer it down on Bolan's ally, but before he could throw the felling blow, the Executioner adjusted his aim and blasted a crater out of the cultist's back, hurling his corpse across the room.

Machida flipped over on his last opponent, raining punches on his enemy while Bolan swung his Uzi back around, hammering out a long staccato burst at a trio of cultists charging up the stairs. Caught in their headquarters, without their body armor, the Black Serpents were far more vulnerable to being cut down by the Executioner's withering fire. As swiftly as they charged up the stairs, they tumbled lifelessly back down, their internal organs mangled by 9 mm flesh shredders.

"Machida! The lantern!" Bolan shouted. He heaved himself and the limp, rag doll corpse of his shield through the splintered railing, finally shattering it with the weight of two bodies and dropping to the floor as more gunfire hammered at the top of the stairs. The Executioner had just ducked out of the path of the Black Serpent's gunfire and landed next to the stunned Zakoji.

Letting his empty Uzi hang, he drew his two captured SIG-Sauer pistols, thrusting them out to full arm's-length extension. The 9 mm rounds barked from the muzzles of the two handguns, punching into Black Serpents and scattering them.

A fireball hurled from the top of the stairs and crashed

against the gun rack, just as Bolan had planned. The flaming lantern blossomed into a roaring flower of orange. Something metallic ruptured, a can of gun-cleaning oil perhaps, increasing the size of the detonation and scattering blazing automatic weapons everywhere.

Bolan turned to face Zakoji. The cult leader snapped a kick hard into the Executioner's jaw, spinning him back around. Slammed into the wall, Bolan dropped one pistol and clawed to maintain his balance.

Fluttering, burning shreds of the blueprints still hovered in the air, spiraling.

"My blueprints!" Zakoji snarled.

Bolan took the momentary lapse in the cult mastermind's attention to push off from the wall, and pistoning a stovepipe long leg into the madman's chest, struck his embroidered serpent right in the face. With a loud thump, Zakoji was lifted off his feet and catapulted a dozen feet from the Executioner.

Bolan swung around with his remaining pistol and was tracking the cult leader with its muzzle when a couple of Black Serpents burst into view from behind the conflagration of the blazing gun rack. Bolan spun, knowing he wouldn't be able to take both of them, but he still triggered the 9 mm pistol and heard the roar of a submachine gun chewing through the confusion.

Machida's Uzi fire rained down on the pair of cultists, cutting them off before they could open fire on Bolan. The Executioner flipped the Yakuza bossman a brief salute, then turned to Zakoji, only to find him missing.

"Machida! Get the hell out of here!" Bolan shouted. "Try to find Honey and the others!"

"But—"

"Move it, soldier!" Bolan snapped.

Machida fired one last burst to keep the heads of the Black

Serpents down, then took off. Bolan took the breather to re-load his pistol and SMG and recover his fallen weapon. A Black Serpent poked his head and gun around a corner, and the Executioner snap aimed, blowing a hole through his face.

Bolan took off for where he'd hurled Zakoji, hoping to pick up the trail.

A storm of machine-gun fire chewed through the roof of the building, sending Black Serpents flying everywhere.

Suddenly, the Executioner was in a whole new war zone.

BOTAN OKUDAIRA SAW, with his night-vision goggles, the dim lights of the compound as if they were bright, verdant flames burning in the night. Bodies scurried under camouflage net-ting that was stretched over buildings and courtyards, obscur-ing the view, but he could tell that the freaks who had disrupted the meeting between Hogan and Machida were re-acting to some form of attack.

"Hit them, Kenji," Okudaira ordered.

Kenji braced himself with the SAW machine gun and trig-gered it. Flames flashed from the muzzle, streaks of laser fire flickering in the night as tracers burned towards the ground. The camouflage netting tore away as he slashed through it with the heavy squad automatic. A couple of the Black Ser-pents below tumbled, smashed to the ground by impacts from 5.56 mm rifle bullets.

More of the cultists reacted, but the JetRanger shuddered as Kenji's pilot triggered the machine-gun pod attached to the far side of the aircraft. Fifty-caliber slugs hammered out in a thunderstorm of wrath that chopped the grounded riflemen, blasting them to gory chunks as 750-grain slugs burst through Kevlar body armor as if it were tissue paper. The Black Ser-pent gunmen were flung limply around the courtyard as the pilot lined up the machine-gun pod and raked the main building with a long, snarling burst that shattered through the concrete walls of the multilevel structure.

The wall cratered, fist-sized chunks ripped out of it by the onslaught, and Okudaira was suitably impressed with the power of the JetRanger's weapons kit. Hogan had excellent taste in firepower, and the helicopter would make a valuable addition to his fleet once he consolidated his power. Indeed, with Kenji's team, and this helicopter, he could wage open war with impunity against other Yakuza clans that dared to defy his will.

"Sir!" Kenji called over his headset. He pointed toward a figure scrambling out a second-story window, firing a submachine gun back the way he'd come.

Okudaira took aim at the man, then froze.

It was Machida, and he was assaulting this compound, seemingly on his own. Black Serpent gunmen surged after him but were slammed back by the Yakuza man's gunfire.

"Give him some cover!" Okudaira ordered, triggering his weapon. Kenji's SAW chattered and cleared out the window.

The cultists were put down handily with a salvo of gunfire that smashed the window-frame.

"Excellent shooting, sir," Kenji said, nodding to his leader.

"You can flatter me later, Kenji. Pilot! Get us close to Machida! Pick him up!" Okudaira ordered.

An explosion rocked the compound, and Okudaira's head snapped around. A rocket trail hung in the air like a column of cotton, looped from the perimeter gate to a spot ten feet from the front door of the main building. Kenji's team had arrived already, taking one of Hogan's off-road capable vehicles to meet the helicopter after the JetRanger paid a visit to the other mercenaries and their aircraft.

They had arrived just in time to start killing Black Serpent defenders armed with antiaircraft missiles, saving Okudaira's life.

He planned to give the survivors among them a bonus, and he sincerely hoped that all of Kenji's trained Yakuza commandos would make it through. If they didn't, then they simply weren't the kind of men he needed in his new, reorganized crime family.

His killer elite were going to make him a force to be reckoned with.

Machida looked stunned as he saw the helicopter hovering just off the rooftop.

"Jump aboard!" Okudaira shouted.

Machida didn't move, his jaw agape.

"Dammit, Machida!" Kenji shouted. He stepped out onto the landing skid, extending a hand to the Yakuza enforcer. "We're sitting ducks up here!"

Hideaki Machida glanced at the courtyard, seeing the roiling carnage burning out of control as the Black Serpents were still recovering in the wake of the twin fists of the JetRanger and Kenji's team making their presence felt. He brought up his Uzi, seemingly on autopilot. This was his chance to help Cooper.

Kenji, stretched out, the SAW hanging from his neckstrap was frozen, stuck in space. Machida raised the Uzi to eye level with one hand and pulled the trigger.

In the same instant, Kenji's head exploded, hot gore splashing across Okudaira's face. Curses filled the air and the helicopter jolted. Machida swung his Uzi, trying to blast the pilot, not knowing if the weapon in his hands could do anything against the mercenary aircraft. Kenji's corpse swan dived off the landing skid onto the roof, his legs draped over the edge.

Gravity took hold of the corpse and dragged it back down to the ground, leaving a slick, glistening trail of dark blood on the rooftop where his cored skull dragged along.

Jolted out of his shock, Machida glanced at the JetRanger as the pilot struggled to swing the nose of the aircraft around. Okudaira hung out the side door, blasting with his machine pistol, but only spraying empty air as the aircraft's rotation threw off his aim. Machida saw the blunt noses of the barrels of the machine-gun pod swinging towards him and took a running leap off the roof. He dropped out of the path of a stream of .50 caliber deathbringers, the cliff wall spewing out a column of pulverised stone where the heavy slugs smashed into it.

Machida hit the ground, his legs flexing to absorb the impact. He staggered backward, off balance. His heel snagged on Kenji's shoulder and he dropped as a second blistering wave of gunfire chewed into the dirt directly in front of him.

A pair of Black Serpents burst into view, firing their weapons into the night sky, trying to bring down the helicopter. One of them shuddered as a rain of bullets punctured his body, throwing his limp form backward as if struck by an invisible baseball bat. The other cultist dived out of the way, skidding in the dirt not far from where Machida had tripped over Kenji's nearly decapitated body.

The cultist and the Yakuza enforcer looked at each other, eyes wide with shock, weapons in hand.

Whoever made the first move would surely be the survivor.

HOGAN SKIDDED TO A HALT as he reached the edge of a smaller cliff. Empty blackness extended into the void beyond his feet, and he called for his fellow mercs to hold up.

The gunman holding Honey Anthony swayed as he came to a halt, the girl kicking and struggling to get free.

"Knock her out and let's go swimming!" Hogan shouted.

Honey lurched over the mercenary's back and tumbled to

the ground. The gunman spun, trying to get hold of the girl once more, but he jerked violently, automatic fire peppering across his chest. Honey curled up, making herself smaller, praying that none of the bullets would drop into her huddled form.

The mercenary, however, snarled in annoyance. His body armor had protected him from all but a flesh wound to his arm, and he struggled to bring his weapon up again to aim at the cultists who were pursuing them. Hogan and the other two mercenaries cut loose as well, laying down a deadly field of fire that would have torn the guts out of any ambushing force. Spread out, with enough of an angle to get behind trees that blocked the fire of their partners, they saturated the forest with streams of 9 mm slugs.

The Black Serpent gunfire died out instantly, but Hogan quickly reloaded.

"Get the girl and let's move!" he ordered, keeping his muzzle aimed at the uncertain shadows of the woods.

A sputter of autofire clipped one of his mercenaries in the head, tossing him to the ground. Hogan dropped to a crouch and scanned for the muzzle blast. There was none, and the head mercenary cursed under his breath.

"Is he okay?" Hogan asked.

"He's still breathing," one of the two remaining gunmen told him. "But he's losing blood fast."

"Son of a bitch," Hogan growled. He eyed Honey, who shuddered in fear. The ugly barrel of his weapon waved at her for a moment. "You've cost me too damn many people!"

Honey tensed. Her fingers dug into the cold, wet forest floor, arms straining to give her the leverage she'd need if she was going to bolt out of the path of a stream of bullets. It wouldn't give her much more than a few more seconds of life, but Honey had fought too hard, gone too damn far to give it up this easily.

"I cost you?" Honey asked. "You're the asshole trying to kidnap me. You're the one trying to kill an FBI agent who got too close to your plan. I cost you? You're blackmailing my father for God knows what!"

"An artillery missile system," Hogan answered. "One of the most up-to-date, low-flying artillery missiles ever developed. It can send a five hundred pound warhead skimming the nape of the earth at an altitude of ten feet. And all small enough to carry three or four in a pickup truck."

"So, a better way for terrorists to destroy cities?" Honey asked.

"A better way for me to make lots of money. More than I'd make saving your worthless hide, bitch," Hogan snapped back.

The ground between Hogan and Honey erupted, leaves and dirt flying as bullets smashed into it. Hogan leaped one way, and Honey sprung in the other, scrambling wildly as the mercenary concentrated on spraying the trees with his weapon. He spun back and fired a burst toward Honey, but she reached the cover of a tree trunk. Slugs hammered into the wood, making the tree shake, but Honey was alive, and she jammed herself tight against the bark, her heart thundering in her ears.

A shape shifted in front of her, and she caught her breath, seeing it duck back behind a trunk.

Was it Cooper? She could only hope, as the mercenaries had proven too much for the Black Serpents to take down. Even if it was Machida, it would still be going from the fire into the frying pan.

Honey saw the flicker of a submachine gun, not far from where the figure disappeared into the shadows. She huddled still, too afraid to even move, and knowing that if she shifted position, Hogan would easily shoot her in the back and kill her. She might even attract attention to the gunman scrambling frantically to save her life. The mercenaries fired again, spraying the darkness where the muzzle-flash erupted, but no groans, no grunts of pain sounded in her ears.

There was still a chance.

If only she had a weapon, if only she could somehow help fight back.

She heard the crunch of boots on leaves and twigs. It could only be Hogan closing in on her, and she imagined him, his weapon aimed at her head, ready to finish off his job. She grabbed at the ground and her hand wrapped around a thick branch. She squeezed the wood, and knew that against a gun, it wouldn't be much.

But it would still give her some ability to fight.

If Hogan wanted to kill her, he'd have to deal with a face full of broken wood first. She hefted the branch. It was heavy. Maybe, just maybe she could beat his brains in before a belly full of bullets put her down for good. She slowly stood up, keeping her back pressed to the tree, awaiting her fate.

THE EXECUTIONER DIVED down the stairs as the .50 caliber slugs pierced the walls of the main compound. Bolan could only hope that the heavy machine gun didn't do any damage to stored chemical or biological weapons. Though the leak would readily solve the problem of the Black Serpents and their threat against Japan, it would also kill Honey, Machida and the remaining Yakuza enforcers.

Bolan hit the steps hard, his muscles taking a beating from the metallic stairs even through the borrowed body armor, but he slid to a stop without feeling anything break. He stumbled slowly to his feet and aimed his Uzi down the next landing. A figure flashed into a doorway below that might have been Zakoji.

Bolan had continued down, realizing that he'd slowed, developing a limp from where his knee barked off the steel edge of a step. It hurt but still supported his weight, and he could feel his foot below the banged knee. At most, it was a bruise, but already, it cut into his speed.

Each slowed step was another foot that Zakoji got ahead, either towards some Armageddon plan of releasing contagion into the valley, or a secret back door into the depths of some cave system that would leave the Executioner hunting him for years to come.

Either way, there could be no escape for the Black Serpent madman. Bolan had to stop him, or thousands of lives were endangered.

The Executioner picked up his pace down the steps, sliding on the railing and letting gravity accelerate him down to the next landing, then finally to the bottom of the base. Each time he landed, his banged-up left knee protested, but that only made Bolan push harder with his right leg to compensate. With each step, his right leg burned with the extra effort placed on it, and he tore through the doorway where Zakoji had disappeared.

Finally, he came to a halt, both legs aflame with pain.

As long as the Executioner's nerves burned with exertion and the sting of bruising, then he was still alive, still capable.

Bolan was ready to finish this fight. He wasn't sure how many more strides he had left in him, how many more minutes of strength to keep him on his feet, to hold his weapons and pull their triggers.

What he stumbled into was a nightmare beyond anything that he could have imagined. The room he encountered was white and brightly lit. It was antiseptic in nature, clean and stark. He had to blink or go blind from the glare. That was not the real horror, though. It was the air lock ahead, and through the air lock, on one wall—windows allowed him to see the nightmare of torn, ragged bodies strewed across the next chamber.

One man in the next room was dead, his head hanging at an odd angle where he sat in the corner. His neck had to have been broken, but before that, his body had been clawed and ravaged by what could only have been the talons of a mindless beast. But closer observation showed that the dead man's fingers were covered in caked blood, his nails splintered and jagged from grinding at his own flesh and digging at the impenetrable walls that held him in.

Bolan saw one survivor was one of Hogan's mercenaries. He had to have been one of the few that had been captured by the Black Serpents. His body armor had been torn off, as had his shirt. Fissures where his fingers had clawed through his own flesh and muscle seeped blood, and his shoulders twitched. His eyes were red rimmed, and his lips were white with frothing foam, as if he were rabid. Along his neck and bared chest, where he had not scratched off the flesh, nodules of red, swollen flesh abounded.

The foaming lips, the nervous twitches and uncontrollable spasms pointed toward rabies. But the buboes that deformed the remaining flesh indicated the plague.

Bolan realized that somehow, Zakoji had found a way to piggyback two deadly diseases into one fast-acting, but slow-killing package that drove its victims mad. The three living people in the next chamber kept their distance from one another, red-rimmed eyes glaring at their fellow occupants with fear. He couldn't hear through the glass, but he could see their lips part, teeth gritting, the foam on their mouths spraying as they hissed angrily at one another.

Dread and pity mingled in the Executioner's heart. Even the mercenary deserved better than to die from whatever satanic cocktail of contagion the Black Serpents whipped up in their deep, dark laboratories.

Bolan tore his eyes from the horror scene and looked for another door. He saw it, and Zakoji slamming it shut. The Executioner charged at the handle, but it was locked.

Then came the hiss of releasing air.

"You must be the descendant, the man who brought down my predecessor four centuries past," a clipped, lightly accented voice spoke in English over the speakers in the clean room. The door that led to the stairwell swung shut and the lock clicked. The Executioner cursed himself for following the madman into a trap.

The air lock door finished hissing and slid slowly open. Alarm bells sounded as the containment area's seal was breached.

"My master and namesake, Lord Zakoji, the great alchemist sorcerer who sought to tear down the corrupt shogunate, swore that you would be defeated in this valley," Zakoji said. "Now, it is I who will be your executioner, not you mine."

Bolan turned and saw the lurching forms of five people stagger through the air lock chamber. Red-rimmed eyes blazed with hatred, feral snarls filling his ears.

The Executioner braced himself, knowing that these zombielike figures would kill him, either with their contagion, or with their blood encrusted, talon hooked fingers.

Innocent lives, destroyed by one madman, were turned into hideous monsters to unleash hell upon an unsuspecting country.

These monsters, however, were going to start with Bolan.

## 16

The Executioner backed away from the figures before him. One man, the captured mercenary, stumbled to the ground. His fingers clawed at the floor as he struggled to right himself.

"Stay where you are!" Bolan ordered. "I can get you medical help. Just stay…"

"It's too late," Aylan said, his voice rasping. Drool strung down from his lips as he spoke, fighting to get back up. "It's too damn late for all of us."

Bolan looked up to the other two. Their red-rimmed eyes flared with madness, for a moment, but their faces were hardly the slack visages of zombies. Instead, there was a sadness to them. "I can help you. Please, just turn around," he said.

"Don't come close," Dylan said hoarsely. "The contagion is spread by parasites."

Bolan kept his Uzi muzzle aimed at them.

Aylan hammered his fist against the tile floor. "The chamber, it's infested with fleas carrying the dual organism. Zakoji explained it to me over the intercom, after I got infected. He managed to fit together the virus that formed rabies to ride along with the bacillus that causes plague. And he spread it through fleas. This version I'm suffering from isn't his final copy, either. The symptoms spring into action almost instantly. I can barely move."

Dylan looked up, his red eyes full of fear. "See, I would be no good, they'd find the infection in me right away. The combo could be contained. But he has a perfected version, one that takes days to incubate. The first victims won't start suffering until long after the fleas carrying the combination have moved on to new hosts, animal or people."

Bolan lowered his weapon. "I'll get you some help," he said.

Racing forward, Bolan pushed the air lock door shut, keeping an eye out for parasites fleeing their hosts. No insectile specks bounded onto the floor of the clean room, the white tiles and the white walls providing a perfect bright background to pick up any wandering creature.

The disease was contained, for the moment.

Looking at the door that Zakoji was hiding behind, he realized one thing. The real disease wasn't contained. The monster who developed the deadly hybrid still lived, and could still escape.

Bolan reloaded his Uzi and emptied the subgun into the locked door that the robed mastermind had hidden himself behind. Wood and metal splintered under a savage assault of 9 mm slugs, and the door swung open slowly, its door handle and lock smashed to bits. The Executioner dropped the empty machine pistol and drew one of his handguns. He went through the doorway and saw the room was empty, a ladder in one corner heading up into the ceiling.

Zakoji had scurried up his bolt-hole.

But the Black Serpent mastermind wouldn't get away for long.

HIDEAKI MACHIDA FACED off with the Black Serpent who had dived for cover, escaping the combined assault of his daiymo

Botan Okudaira's helicopter and his killer elite enforcers. The Black Serpent compound came under attack, presumably because the Yakuza boss, Okudaira, wanted Colin Anthony's blueprints. The ones he had kidnapped Rebecca Anthony to ransom.

Machida watched the Black Serpent guard as he quivered, face-to-face, gunpoint to gunpoint with him.

"We can kill each other, or you can get away from this carnage," Machida told him. "Your choice."

The Black Serpent guard looked toward the sounds of gunfire and explosions shattering the compound, then back at Machida. The battered and tattered Yakuza man kept his gun trained on the cultist, who rose, and ran toward the chain fence perimeter. Machida sighed with relief and had started to get up when a blast of gunfire cut down the Black Serpent as he was halfway up the fence.

Machida scurried, pressed tighter against the wall. He reloaded his weapon and looked over to see a single Okudaira enforcer, dressed in commando black, race into view. Machida aimed for the legs and swept the gunman's thighs with a salvo of flesh ripping bullets. The Yakuza thug smashed into the ground, his assault rifle flying from numbed fingers.

Machida closed in on the injured man and fired another burst into the back of the wounded gunner's head. Okudaira's killer elite slumped, his gore flowing like a river into the dirt at Machida's feet.

Machida turned and scooped up the fallen assault weapon, an M-16 with a 100-round extended drum. He didn't know how many shots were in it, but it was still worth the extra firepower. From the weight of the rifle, it seemed to be fully loaded. Just to be sure, the Machida patted down the dead man, pulling spare magazines off the corpse.

The rifle would cut through body armor more quickly and

efficiently, making all the difference in the world. He wasn't the best shot, and aiming for the head wouldn't be possible in a race against death.

He looked around the corner and gazed upon hell on earth. The Black Serpents had been swept aside by scythes of automatic weapons fire, their corpses strewed bonelessly about the compound. Flames roared in various smaller buildings, and the camouflage netting disintegrated as the blaze devoured it hungrily. Well-equipped and armored commandos spread out around the corpses, kicking bodies and firing point-blank into anything that showed a sign of reaction.

Machida did a quick count of Okudaira's commandos. There were eight of them.

Eight, and the helicopter, that hovered over the scene, swirling up dust devils of glowing orange clouds, underlit by the raging fires blazing throughout the compound. Machida shouldered the M-16 and aimed at the helicopter.

He had one chance to take out the Yakuza boss, and if he failed, he'd have eight trained killers charging his position.

Or just firing their weapons dry, killing him where he stood.

Machida knew that for the good of his clan, he'd have to try. He was a man of honor and loyalty, but Okudaira hadn't done one thing to earn his fealty other than to step in after murdering the previous daimyo. He put the ring front sight of the M-16 on the JetRanger as it swung around, the pilot scanning, possibly for him. Machida sighted on the Plexiglas dome and pulled the trigger.

The M-16 was an entirely new experience for the Yakuza man. The rifle kicked powerfully against his arm, the full-auto stream of bullets coming out the other end spiking the stock hard against his shoulder, threatening to wrench the gun out of his hands or pull him off target with the force of recoil.

Machida leaned his weight into the assault rifle, continuing to direct a spray of 5.56 mm slugs into the cockpit of the JetRanger.

The helicopter lurched violently, and Machida ducked back as the first burps of return fire from Okudaira's killer elite lanced at him. A dust storm flew up as enemy projectiles chewed stone and dirt, creating a swirling, violent cloud that the Yakuza man was momentarily grateful for. He was hidden, and he heard the helicopter slam into the ground, metal bending and warping as gravity crushed the aircraft.

"You have cleared the way for your family to return to honor," Machida said to himself softly. "Now, just to live to see its return to that glory."

He fumbled with the magazine in the M-16's well, prying it free when he finally discovered the magazine catch. It took a few frantic moments to paw another loaded clip into the weapon, and the dust cloud continued to churn and swirl at the corner of the main building. In his peripheral vision, he saw the flame lit shadows of men dance across the column of flying dust and debris, warning him of the imminent approach of at least a few of Okudaira's trained murderers.

Machida swung the M-16 and fired into the cloud. One of the enforcers stepped right into the blazing path of hypersonic projectiles, the bullets slicing through the unsuspecting killer at over 3000 feet per second. Perforated a half dozen times, his insides churned to mush by the tumbling motion of the unstable slugs, Okudaira's assassin slammed to a halt as if he'd hit an invisible brick wall, blood gushing from his nose and mouth.

A curse filled the air as at least one other man dived away from Machida's autofire blast. Machida hit the ground as a rifle muzzle poked around the corner and erupted. Bullets tore through the air where he'd been standing in only moments before. Machida swung up the muzzle of his rifle and pulled the trigger, but only succeeded in peppering the wall with fresh pockmarks. The lone Yakuza man braced himself against the commandos, knowing that they would come again, using more effective methods. All he had left was to stay low, as small a target as possible, and keep shooting until his weapons ran dry.

He shrugged the Uzi to his side, ready pick it up when the larger rifle emptied, and set his pistol on the ground in front of him. If this was going to be his last stand, he would not die as a deer, but as a tiger.

Suddenly, a black, shadowy form loomed over his head. Gunfire rattled, and from the sound of surprised screams, he knew that the man up top had just caught Okudaira's elite killers off guard. Machida whispered a silent thanks to Special Agent Matt Cooper, and stuffed his handgun back into its holster before clambering to his feet.

He looked up and was stunned to see the robed silhouette of Master Zakoji standing atop the ledge. He held a canister in one arm, shiny and silver with the bright yellow-and-red emblem of biohazard displayed on its side. Zakoji looked down and chuckled.

"You have all come to steal the victory of Burakku Uwibami?" he called out. He held up the silver canister, orange glints playing off its shiny reflective surfaces from the fires raging in the compound.

"You fools! I am the Lord Zakoji, master alchemist and sorcerer reborn! I am he who will fulfill the promises of more than four centuries, to bring Japan's corrupted, impure form to its knees to rise again from the ashes! And if I have to release my cleansing plague here and now, and succumb to my own weapon, then so be it!"

"No!" Machida snarled, bringing up his M-16.

Suddenly, a black missile of human flesh slammed into Za-koji from behind, two bodies sailing into the firelit space over the compound's courtyard.

The Executioner had finally caught up with the madman.

RHODE HOGAN STEPPED into view, his weapon aiming at Re-becca Anthony, but before he could pull the trigger, she cut loose with a swing worthy of a baseball star. The length of wood in her hands shattered against Hogan's shoulder, glancing off it and cushioning some of the force that continued on to strike the mercenary in the head. He staggered backwards grinding his wrist across his eyes to wipe splinters away, cursing and snarling as he fired an uncontrolled burst at the ground.

Honey cringed, turning away. Instead of avoiding the blind salvo of Parabellum bullets emptied at the ground, she caught a bullet through her thigh, the tender flesh parting before the blistering projectile. Honey crashed to the ground with a shriek, and Hogan brought his wrist back down from his eyes.

"Not so tough now, eh, bitch?" Hogan snapped.

Honey glanced up at the murderous, hate-filled killer. His temple was slashed by a jagged end of the club she broke against him, and his eyes were red and livid from the splinters and dust that issued from the broken branch. His hand was unsteady as he took aim with his automatic weapon.

Honey threw the remaining end of the branch with a strength born of desperation. Again, Hogan's gunfire flew wild as wood clunked off his forehead. Automatic weapons fire lit up the night in the woods behind her, and she glanced back.

Maybe, just maybe, Unno had recovered from that hit to the head. His eyes had seemed alert, and he was still breathing when she rushed to his side. Someone was still fighting tooth and claw with the last of Hogan's mercenaries.

The bullet-headed killer, his face a glistening, bloody mask where she'd split his forehead, growled with savage fury. He had to have dropped his gun, because he was charging at her, blunt fingers extended like claws to tear at her.

Honey kicked up frantically with her good leg, her appropriated combat boot striking the mercenary in the jaw. Her entire leg went numb as 250 pounds of muscle slammed against her, but the wild swing of her foot had done its work. Hogan, instead of landing on her and wrapping those huge, callused hands around her throat, had smashed into the tree, thrown off his course. Both legs racked with pain, Honey clawed herself backward. Though fresh flaming agony shot through her with each push of her feet against the ground, she knew that if she didn't keep retreating from the infuriated soldier of fortune, she would never feel any pain again.

Hogan stumbled and crawled on all fours after her, his teeth bared in a rictus of anger that Honey never thought possible in a human face. This was no man, anymore, this was a bloodthirsty beast, a killing machine that would only be satisfied when her head and shoulders were crushed to a pulp, or her skull torn from her neck. Honey kicked again, but the pain of the bullet wound through her thigh sapped the strength of the blow. Hogan's face was stamped by her boot sole, but he kept coming, one powerful hand gripping her ankle and twisting hard.

Honey screamed as she felt her bones grind together in the enraged killer's fist, and she leaned forward, her fingers clawing at his wrist. She sank her nails deep into his rough skin, but even as blood flushed to the surface, Hogan snagged one of her hands and pulled her even closer to him. Honey screamed again, this time not in pain, but in the same kind of savage, animal rage that had possessed the mercenary.

"I've had enough of you!" Honey screamed, and she raked

Hogan's face with her free hand. Blood and skin came away under her nails as the mercenary wailed, his eye ravaged by her clawing strike. With a brutal twist, the big man yanked her off balance and hammered her in the head with a fist that felt like a boulder.

Eyes unfocused by the impact, Honey tried to raise her free hand to block a second punch, but the murderous commando blew through her defenses and smashed her nose, gouts of blood pouring down into her mouth and threatening to choke her. Honey thrashed, spitting up blood and curses as she flailed. She didn't have the strength, though, nor the skill to match her will to fight and took another punch in the jaw. Her head snapped around and lights flashed in her brain.

She was going to die, and there was nothing more she could do about it. Honey struggled to hang on to consciousness when Hogan suddenly lurched.

Through her blurred eyes, she saw the stumbling form of Unno, hacking down again and again with the frame of his weapon, hammering irresistable steel against the skull of the enraged mercenary. Squirts of gore splattered across Honey's face, and as she blinked away the blood, she was able to see Unno more clearly. His torn and injured face was contorted and twisted, reddened by streaks of his own vital fluids and further sprayed with the messy splashes every time he pounded down into Hogan's softening, mushy skull.

Honey tried to push herself up, to speak, but it was one or the other, and she barely had the presence of mind for any words. She sat up as Unno kicked Hogan's corpse to the forest floor. Then, pulling his handgun out, he emptied the weapon into the nearly headless figure, muzzle-flashes lighting his enraged features. He kept pulling the trigger, even after no more bullets were left in the gun, jerking the pistol with each tug for long, agonizing seconds until sanity seemed to once again emerge.

"Unno?" Honey asked, finally recovering her own ability to speak.

The Yakuza enforcer looked at her, eyes still sparking wildly with bloodlust, but he struggled to bring himself back under control. He let the empty pistol drop free from his fingers and his legs gave out. Honey crawled closer to him as he struggled to rise to his elbows.

"Unno?" Honey spoke to him again.

"You okay?" the Japanese gangster asked.

"I can't walk," Honey groaned.

"I don't think I can, either," Unno replied. He smiled weakly. "Let's just lay down here for a while."

Honey nodded numbly. "That's a real good idea."

Honey and Unno lay in the grass, recovering their strength, hoping that someone would come looking for them both.

As MACK BOLAN RODE Zakoji to the ground, he took in the battleground around him. Burned buildings and corpses lay strewed about, like the aftermath of some giant's rampage. A crumpled helicopter sat to one side, and scrambling black-clad commandos scurried away from the falling duo.

The stainless-steel biohazard containment unit had dropped and bounced away as the two battling opponents hit the ground. The collision threw Bolan and Zakoji apart, their bodies rolling and tumbling. The Executioner lurched to his feet first and pulled out his pistol. He didn't want to risk blowing a hole in the biohazard container with a stray shot.

Pistol in hand, the Executioner rose quickly and saw Zakoji dive behind the frame of the crashed helicopter. Bolan chased the fleeing madman with a 9 mm bullet, but the slug only pinged off the metal hull of the downed aircraft.

The side door of the JetRanger kicked open and a figure crawled out of the cabin, spraying bullets wildly from a submachine gun. The newcomer was screaming in Japanese, and half his face was caked in blood from a viscious cut on his forehead. Still, the Executioner recognized the man's round face, the thick, powerful arms and shoulders under his skin-tight night suit. He was familiar with the close cropped fuzz on a domelike skull.

It was Botan Okudaira, the very man he'd come all the way to Japan to stop.

"Christmas comes early," Bolan mused as he swung the front sight of the SIG-Sauer and blasted away with a trio of bullets. The daimyo jerked violently against the side of the crashed JetRanger, gurgling up blood. The hammering of the machine pistol stopped, and it slipped from the gangster's lifeless fingers, striking the dirt long before he did.

Bolan's shoulders sagged. After fighting nonstop for hours through hordes of mobsters, mercenaries and madmen, to have Okudaira plop into his lap was almost a disappointment. Still, he was glad it was easy as it was. He was ready to collapse.

"Cooper!" Machida shouted.

Bolan spun and kicked from the spot he was standing in, instincts hurling him out of the path of a wave of automatic fire eminating from the deadly elite guard of the man he'd just shot. Swinging the pistol around, still in midair, he caught two gunmen with four shots. One spasmed, but stayed standing, his body armor protecting him. The other assassin flopped over, a boneless mass of unfeeling flesh.

The Executioner hit the ground and rolled to Okudaira's feet. Machida retreated, firing around the corner as the killer elite focused on him as well. The M-16 he fired produced a blazing muzzle-flash that attracted far more attention than Bolan's little 9 mm pistol. Scooping up Okudaira's MP-5, Bolan tore a spare magazine off the dead man's vest and slammed it into the empty weapon.

Between the two men, they cleared Okudaira's assassins in a deadly cross fire that cut down the black-clad gunmen in a matter of moments.

Machida stepped cautiously out into the open, fumbling to reload his assault rifle, looking to Bolan.

"Was that the last of them?" Bolan asked.

"I counted only eight active," Machida answered. "But it doesn't pay to relax."

Bolan reached for another magazine off Okudaira's corpse. "Especially not with Zakoji still at large."

The Executioner was in midreload when he sensed a shape sizzling through the air. Feet impacted hard against his shoulders and threw him to the ground, knocking his weapon from his hands. Zakoji hopped forward, the ribbon of his katana glimmering in the firelight as he charged toward Machida.

Bolan struggled to get up, sucking breath back into his lungs after having the air knocked out of him. He looked up and saw the cult leader cross the distance between Bolan and Machida in the instant that it took the Yakuza man to drop his rifle and claw for his handgun.

Machida never stood a chance as Zakoji swept his blade edge across the man's chest. The Kevlar parted, but the Yakuza man managed to step out of the reach of most of the cut. However, his pistol was lost, ripped from his grasp as steel clanked on steel.

Bolan lurched to his feet, reaching for his handgun. In the dive for Okudaira's corpse, however, he had lost the weapon. Now the only thing he had left was the sword he'd brought with him. And the throwing knives.

The Executioner sailed one blade, point first, into Zakoji's shoulder. The Black Serpent mastermind snarled and spun, facing Bolan, hatred in his eyes as the American raised his own sword up to the challenge.

"Sword to sword," Zakoji snarled, deflecting the Executioner's first cut.

Bolan backpedaled and barely stopped the madman's return stroke, blades ringing in a clash of flowing metal.

Zakoji smirked. "Taste defeat at the hands of Zakoji. Are you ready to fall, man in black?"

Bolan flashed in, but Zakoji's defense was too good, blocking three rapid strokes with effortless grace. The cultist's blade tip came close enough to slice open the front of the Executioner's body armor. Another step closer, and Bolan would have easily been gutted. Instead, the Executioner managed to frantically block the next few blows, but each of Zakoji's sword strokes took their toll, the ferocity of the slashes numbing the Bolan's arms even as he blocked them.

Zakoji's rage had faded to bored confidence. He seemed to merely be flicking the tip of his sword like a wand, but he struck with strength enough to put the larger man off balance. Machida suddenly lunged into view and lashed wildly with his own blade.

Zakoji winced as the katana sliced across his back, but the cut was too shallow, only skin deep. The robe split wide open, skin slick with blood as the madman turned his back to Bolan and drove the point of his own sword deep into Machida's belly.

"No!" the Executioner growled, seeing the Yakuza man stiffen, then grip Zakoji's robe.

"Now, Cooper!" the gravely wounded gangster shouted.

Zakoji struggled to rip himself free, but only turned to see the firelit glint of Bolan's katana arc across his vision. He furrowed his brow and tried to command the rest of his body to act, when he felt himself slipping, tumbling.

Bolan looked at the impossible angle of Zakoji's neck as he hit the dirt. He rushed to Machida's side, catching him as he slipped to the ground.

Machida looked at the sword handle poking from his belly, and winced.

"I should have gotten closer," he said with a cough.

"Don't talk. I can call for help. I can stabilize the bleeding," Bolan said.

"It is too late, Cooper," Machida said. Large, black eyes looked at him imploringly.

Machida snorted and blood poured from his nostrils. He ignored the spurt, licked his lips and looked back up to the American. "He boasted that you would taste defeat today, Executioner."

Bolan frowned.

"He was wrong," Machida concluded.

"No, Hideaki," Bolan answered. "I watched a good man die today."

Machida smiled sadly. In a different lifetime, who knew, they could have been friends, brothers fighting for the same cause.

"Thank you, Cooper," he said softly. Then he closed his eyes.

Bolan took a deep breath, then lowered the man's head gingerly to the ground.

He struggled to his feet, his body aching. He glanced toward the front gate where two people stepped into view.

He instantly recognized the limping forms of Honey Anthony and the Yakuza street soldier called Unno. Bolan looked back down to Machida, not speaking. Honey chewed her lower lip, trying to hold back tears. Unno let out a mournful moan.

"Hogan?" Bolan asked the two.

"Dead," Honey answered, her voice cracking, on the verge of tears.

The Executioner had only one more thing to do. He searched for a radio to call for help for the survivors.

# VANISHING POINT

**A U.S. aircraft carrier carrying a top secret weapon is hijacked in the Pacific....**

The USS *Stennis* has been hijacked and on board is the X-51—the most advanced unmanned aircraft ever built. As the carrier becomes a war zone and the crew succumbs to a poison attack, a covert three-man unit called Able Team is the last line of defense against a global shock wave.

# STONY MAN ®

## #82

*Available April 2006 at your favorite retail outlet.*

# James Axler
## Outlanders®

Reborn as neogods, an anient race
begins its final conquest in...

# RIM OF THE WORLD
### Outlanders #37

An ancient artifact claimed to unlock secrets hidden for two
thousand years and restore the control of a ruthless Sumerian
god has the Cerebus warriors battling blood-thirsty rebels in their
determination to prevent such a destiny.

**Available May 2006 at your favorite retail outlet.**

GOUT37

# THE DESTROYER™

## #143

**America's health system is going to the dogs...**

# BAD DOG

**In an effort to prevent skyrocketing health premiums, the president of the Institute of Nationalized Humane Health Care has started using trained dogs to snuff out costly, disease-carrying people. Remo must stop the dog attacks at the source—by eliminating the elusive, mysterious dog handler himself.**

*Available April 2006 at your favorite retail outlet.*

# DEATH LANDS®

## JAMES AXLER

### Labyrinth

In a ruined world, the past and the future
clash with frightening force…

**NO TIME TO LOSE**
It took only minutes for human history to derail
in a mushroom cloud—now more than a century later, whatever destiny lies ahead for humanity is
bound by the rules that have governed survival since the dawn of time: part luck, part skill and part
hard experience. For Ryan Cawdor and his band, survival in Deathlands means keeping hold of what
you have—or losing it along with your life.

**BORN TO DIE**
In the ancient canyons of New Mexico, the citizens of Little Pueblo prepare to sacrifice Ryan and his
companions to ancient demons locked inside a twentieth-century dam project. But in a world where
nuke-spawned predators feed upon weak and strong alike, Ryan knows avenging eternal spirits
aren't part of the game. Especially when these freaks spit yellow acid—and their creators are the
whitecoat masterminds of genetic recombination, destroyed by their mutant offspring born of sin and
science gone horribly wrong.…

In the Deathlands, some await a better tomorrow, but others hope it never comes.…